"What do you want with me?"

She tried to step around him, clutching a satchel to her chest.

"You may be in danger, Ginny. The police aren't sure where that stun grenade that was thrown last night came from and who it was meant for."

"I appreciate your concern, but I don't feel like I'm in danger."

"Then why do you keep looking over your shoulder?"

"I–" She broke off, her eyes unfocused.

Colin knew that look. She was scared. "It's going to be all right." He tried to smile to put her at ease, but the gesture felt tight. "I'd like to look out for you."

"I don't need a babysitter." She sidestepped him and walked away.

If the Secret Service had taught him anything, it was that threats lurked where you least expected them.

And he was right. She opened the car door, and the loud roar of an engine springing to life nearby sent him into alert.

And then he saw it. A white van sped down the parking lot aisle, right for Ginny.

Michelle Karl is an unabashed bibliophile and romantic suspense author. She lives in Canada with her husband and an assortment of critters, including a codependent cat and an opinionated parrot. When she's not reading and consuming copious amounts of coffee, she writes the stories she'd like to find in her "to be read" pile. She also loves animals, world music and eating the last piece of cheesecake.

Books by Michelle Karl

Love Inspired Suspense

Fatal Freeze
Unknown Enemy

UNKNOWN
ENEMY

MICHELLE KARL

HARLEQUIN® LOVE INSPIRED® SUSPENSE

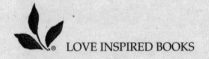

LOVE INSPIRED BOOKS

Recycling programs
for this product may
not exist in your area.

ISBN-13: 978-0-373-67754-2

Unknown Enemy

Copyright © 2016 by Faith Boughan

www.Harlequin.com

Printed in U.S.A.

I will praise Thee; for I am fearfully and wonderfully made:
marvellous are Thy works;
and that my soul knoweth right well.
—*Psalms* 139:14

For Emily Z
May your translating never be fraught with peril
But if it is, I've got your back

ONE

Virginia Anderson pushed back from the desk with a sigh, rubbing her tired eyes with a thumb and index finger. If she had to spend another hour in Rhoads, Pennsylvania's Gwyn Ponth College library without seeing the fading October sunlight, she'd go stark raving mad. *Of course,* she thought, *I have at least three more hours of documents to pore through, so what will* that *make me?*

Taking the work home? Not an option. The combination of futon, fleece blanket, tea and heavy reading would put her right to sleep. Better to sit on a hard chair in a cool, quiet library and actually get her reading done.

"See you tomorrow, Ginny?"

Virginia—Ginny, to most everyone save her parents—waved at Donna, Gwyn Ponth College's head librarian. "I'll stick around until Roger comes in to start cleaning."

Donna tut-tutted and shook her head. "You

work too much, my dear. You part-timers aren't paid nearly enough for the amount of hours you put in each and every day. If you're not teaching, here you are. Don't you ever sleep? You have a big meeting tomorrow, yes?"

"I only sleep if I have to." Ginny laughed, waving Donna out the door. "Plus, it's a meeting with a stuffy old grump from the museum. If I play it right, by this time next year I'll have a tenure-track position and have made the historical discovery of a lifetime, and the lack of sleep will have been worth it."

Donna swept out the door with a sympathetic smile. "I certainly hope so. Tell Roger I said hello."

A smile crept into the corners of Ginny's mouth. Since mid-September, Donna and one of the custodians had been leaving brief, affectionate notes and messages for each other through Ginny, though she'd never actually seen the head librarian and Roger meet in person. If only she could arrange it somehow, but Roger wasn't a very chatty guy. He was a little on the shy side, and had a hard time making eye contact with others. It explained his hesitance to court the librarian in person, but Ginny was happy to be the go-between for them. It was sweet, and she thought Donna and Roger would make a cute couple.

As Ginny focused once more on the journal article in front of her, the lights in the room turned off with an audible click. Had Donna turned them off by accident, out of habit? "Not again, Dee," she called. No response. The librarian must have left in a hurry. "Never mind, I'll get it."

This section of the library book stacks was dim enough to cause eye strain when all the lights were on, let alone having only the light from the emergency exit signs and the intruding outside light from streetlamps to navigate by. As she approached the light switch, a thump came from somewhere behind her. It sounded close. Had she left one of her books too close to the edge of the table?

"Hello?" Ginny squinted into the darkness of the book stacks behind her. "Is someone there?"

The sound of a pen hitting the floor sent her flying in the direction of the light switch. She felt a looming presence behind her just as a hand tapped her shoulder.

"Hey, kid," said a gruff voice behind her. "Think you're smart, hiding in here? Don't make another move."

Don't move? Ginny knew there were still other people in the building, few as they might be, so she made the obvious choice. She shouted and twisted away as the hand slid off her shoulder, flailing her palms against the wall, fingers groping for the light switch.

With a click, the lights flickered on and relief flooded into Ginny's limbs. She shot forward, bracing herself against the end of the nearest bookshelf. Her fingers brushed the spine of a hardcover book. She yanked it off the shelf and whirled around, swinging the book at what she assumed was her attacker's head.

"Hey, stop!" He covered his head with his arms as the book made contact, then reached out and snatched the book away from her. He tossed it aside and held his hands up. "I'm not after you—I thought you were a student trying to sneak around in here off-hours. I can see now you're not a student."

Ginny grabbed another book and held it aloft, ready to throw it and run if he took another step closer. "I don't believe you. Who are you? Why did you creep up on me in the dark instead of talking like a normal person?" His shirt bore the college crest and he looked too old to be an undergraduate—early thirties, maybe—but his coal-dark hair and razor stubble said *troublemaker*.

He raised one obsidian eyebrow as the sound of another book hitting the floor echoed from somewhere deep inside the library stacks. "Instinct due to training, plus I didn't want to give you a chance to run off and disappear elsewhere. Earlier today, I heard we're having some issues with students trying to hide in the archival area overnight. Something about accessing the controlled documents for their projects without the hassle of being monitored by a librarian. But we can discuss that later. Get down."

"Why should I?"

"Trust me, please." He reached for her arm and pulled her down into a crouch.

She drew back from his grip and scooted a few feet away from him, ready to demand he tell her what was going on, but his attention had fixated elsewhere and off of her. He had one finger to his lips. Stay quiet, really? After all that?

"Is there another way out of here?" He kept his voice low. "A back door?"

Ginny frowned, the words spilling out before she could help herself. "Haven't you been in the library before at all?"

"I'm new," he growled. "So, is there?"

Ginny swallowed, hoping she didn't say anything else that could be construed as careless. Clearly, the man thought they were in danger, but he'd been the one waiting in the dark, hadn't he? What if he had used this moment to divert her attention and was planning something horrible? What if he had a partner waiting in the book stacks to abduct her the moment she let her guard down? He hadn't given her a good enough reason to trust him. As much as she hated to leave her wallet and research notes in the library, she might lose precious escape seconds by taking the time to grab either one.

Taking a deep breath, Ginny visualized the back door that led to the library's administrative offices, said a quick prayer and silently counted down from three.

When she reached zero, she pushed off the floor and bolted toward freedom.

Seriously? Colin Tapping groaned as the woman sprinted away from him. She had no idea what kind of danger she might be putting herself in. The best-case scenario was that a student had, in fact, shut the lights off and hidden in the library in hopes of working here through the night. But his former line of work as a Secret Service agent had taught him to never underestimate the potential dangers of a situation.

Doing so risked lives. He'd learned that the hard way and he'd vowed to never let it happen again. Not that he'd thought he'd ever be in that kind of situation again, and especially not on a college campus in the middle of small-town America.

He rushed after her, listening for footsteps, thumps or anything else that sounded out of place in a library. Would she be headed for the front door? The college library had a simple floor plan, so there couldn't be more than a few exits for her to choose from.

The library's front entrance was dim and empty, with no movement from any of the doors at the main exit. He couldn't have been more than a few seconds behind her, and those doors were heavy and slow to close. She hadn't left this way. Might there be another entrance and exit for library staff? Colin took a left turn and ran past the ground level's odd contrast of modern cubicles containing student computer terminals and glass cases displaying old, rare books. When he reached the hallway containing staff offices, he heard the tap of shoes on laminate flooring, followed by a feminine shout of dismay.

Colin reached a bend in the hallway to find the woman he'd followed kneeling on the floor, crouched over another prone figure with dark, curly hair. He took two steps toward them, already pulling his cell phone out of his pocket to dial 911, and froze.

A black cylindrical device rolled into the hallway from around the corner at the other end. It bounced against the side wall and skipped toward them.

"Get out of there!" Colin shouted at the woman. She turned to regard him with wide, frightened eyes, but she hadn't yet seen the grenade. "Grenade! Run to me!"

Fright morphed from confusion to alarm, but instead of running toward him, she lost a precious half second by glancing at the person on the floor. Colin knew that look—she wanted to save her friend, but knew she didn't have the strength to carry the person.

And in that lost moment, Colin knew it was too late.

The grenade exploded with a concussive bang. Colin collapsed where he stood as a bright white light flooded all his senses. He closed his eyes and counted to five. When he opened them, his vision had begun to return.

Relief poured through every inch of his body, and the flood of adrenaline at realizing he was still alive shot him to his feet. *Only a stun grenade...but I guess it wasn't a student hiding in the stacks after all.*

Colin stumbled toward the blonde woman

and the prone figure, his ears ringing. She was blinking and shaking her head, trying to restore her vision and hearing. He wanted to tell her that her hearing would return within the next few hours, but she might have some ongoing discomfort for a few days. Tinnitus was always a possibility after being hit with a stun grenade. He reached for her shoulder, and she startled at his touch.

When she made eye contact, Colin swayed where he knelt before recovering his senses. She was stunningly gorgeous, with piercing blue eyes and long blond hair that framed her face. Her features reminded him of the images of runway models he'd seen in the newspaper—angular, perfectly proportioned, feminine. Combined with the display of compassion for her friend, it had a powerful impact, and Colin's heart was overtaxed. He thought he felt it skip a beat before he regained control of the moment.

He lifted his thumb up for a moment and then turned it down. If she had an injury, they'd deal with that first. She gave him a thumbs-up in return and gestured to the person lying on the floor. Colin now recognized her as the middle-aged woman who'd given him a library tour on his first day of teaching on campus.

"Hurt?" Colin said, though of course neither of them could hear each other.

The younger woman leaned over and touched two fingers to the back of the librarian's skull. Her fingers came away wet and red. Tears filled her eyes and he resisted the urge to let his emotions take over and offer comfort. His sympathy went out to her, but calling emergency services took priority.

He dialed 911 and repeated their location and the nature of the emergency five times, since he couldn't hear the person on the other end to know if anyone had even picked up yet. Finally, he ended with a simple instruction. "Three subjects hit by stun grenade, hearing lost. Repeat, I cannot hear. If you have received this message, please redial this number after I hang up."

He hung up and waited, counting the seconds until his phone lit up. When it did, he released the breath he'd been holding, thanked the person on the other end and turned his attention back to the two women. And here he'd thought teaching criminology classes in a small college would be a break from the exhausting Secret Service life. This was the exact thing he'd come here to get away from after making a career-ending mistake two years ago. Last spring, he'd realized staying in Washington, DC, wasn't doing him any favors. He needed to move on and forget about the ache of being dismissed—and the regret of making a mistake that had caused the woman he loved to be killed, thanks to his inability to separate his heart from his job.

How did he not know the name of the woman in front of him? Shouldn't he have seen her around by now? Gwyn Ponth was quite small, so far as local colleges went.

She checked the other woman's pulse, and a second wave of relief flooded through his veins when her worried frown eased. Gently, he helped her to roll the librarian onto her back. She remained unconscious, breath labored but steady, and Colin checked around her head for the source of the blood matting her hair. It appeared to be a superficial wound, much to his great relief. The librarian would feel terrible for a few weeks and likely suffer frustrating headaches, but she'd live.

It was then that Colin noticed the younger woman's tremble, tears of fright slipping down her cheeks despite the resolve set in her jaw. Her long hair fell in curtains on each side of her face, and from this angle, her delicate features carried an intriguing, ethereal symmetry.

An errant tear escaped its prison and slipped down the side of her right cheek. Without thinking, Colin reached out to wipe it away. Surprise swept through him as he brushed his thumb across her cheek toward her hair. Where he'd expected smooth skin, he felt the tight, bumpy dryness of skin damage—burn scarring? Some other injury?

Instantly, she gasped and knocked his hand away with enough force to sting. The motion revealed too-shiny, reddish scarring from the outside corner of her eye down to the midcenter of her jaw. Her hair had covered it completely.

She scrambled to her feet and leaned against the far side of the hall, where she stayed until the paramedics and police arrived on scene. Once they could both hear again, he'd apologize properly.

And find out if she knew of anybody who might want her or the librarian dead.

TWO

The next morning, Ginny arrived at work a half hour early, despite the department head's insistence that she take the rest of the week off. Her hearing was still a little muffled, but nothing that she needed to lie in bed over. One of the Language and Culture Department's teaching assistants had been assigned to take over her classes for the week—and she'd sent the lesson plans in early this morning—but Ginny had a meeting scheduled for today that nothing short of forced hospitalization could keep her from. Unfortunately for Donna, the head librarian's injury had been more serious, and she was still hospitalized. The doctors had allowed Ginny to go home after getting checked over last night.

As Ginny checked her work email, the memory of finding Donna lying bleeding on the floor was replaced by that of the shocked visage of the handsome man who'd accosted her in the library and helped her after the stun grenade. All that, and she hadn't even learned his name.

Curious, she loaded up the Gwyn Ponth website and scrolled through to the faculty page. "All right. Who are you?"

"I'm not sure who you're actually looking for on there, but I'm Colin Tapping. A little farther down the page, though."

Alarmed, Ginny spun in her chair. The man from last night stood in her office doorway, arms crossed. "Uh...hello?"

He glanced around the shoe box–sized office. "I've owned refrigerators larger than this."

"I spend most of my time in the library or teaching, and they give the best offices to tenured professors." She stood, matching his stance. "But I doubt you're here to talk about office space."

He extended his hand and she reluctantly accepted, feeling an unpleasant gnawing of anxiety in the pit of her stomach. He'd touched her scarred face when trying to wipe away a tear last night. In the process, he'd unknowingly brushed aside the hair she always wore down to cover up the disfigurement her cheek had suffered in a car crash twenty years ago. That crash had effectively ended what her mother had thought would be a lucrative and fame-driven modeling career for her daughter. Her mother had never hidden her desire to live vicariously through her daughter's success, after her own career had tanked years prior. Her mother had never said it outright, but Ginny had always suspected she was the cause of her mother's career tanking. After all, an unexpected pregnancy in an early marriage would certainly complicate a modeling career.

"I'm Colin Tapping. Teaching in the Criminology Department this semester." His handshake was firm and strong. "Though not for the rest of the week. I assume the college insisted the same for you?"

"As you can see, it didn't stick. I'm Ginny Anderson, specialist in ancient languages and history. I don't recall seeing you at the faculty briefing before the semester began."

He pulled his hand back from hers and leaned against the door frame. His eyes flicked to the side of her face and back, but not fast enough to escape her notice. She felt her cheeks grow warm and she touched her hair, making sure it covered the scar. After the car crash, Ginny's mother had let her know, in no uncertain terms, that Ginny's beauty— which her mother had bitterly pointed out at a family gathering was her daughter's only true redeeming quality—had been unequivocally lost forever, and thusly she would never really amount to much.

Ginny didn't talk to her mother much anymore, but she'd worked hard to make a career for herself teaching and studying ancient history and linguistics. She'd become a specialist in ancient languages, and this morning's meeting with the local history museum's curator would bring her one step closer to securing a future at the college. A tenure-track position was up for grabs this year, and if she proved herself valuable enough to the college's reputation to earn it, she'd be placed on the list of teachers eligible for a permanent tenure position after a few years of hard work. While there were at least six part-time professors vying for tenure track within the department, rumor had it the department head was leaning toward securing someone with a wide range of specializations in both language and history. Ginny shared this qualification with one other professor in the department, though she hadn't yet formally met her. She only knew it was a woman who'd been a late hire to the faculty after the abrupt departure of the school's Italian history and language professor.

"I was a last-minute addition to the team."

Ginny waited for him to elaborate, but he

said nothing. She leaned over her computer and began scrolling again through the list of faculty members at the college. If he wouldn't explain, maybe his bio on the website would.

A chuckle escaped as he must have realized her intentions. "I'm former Secret Service. I don't know what they've put in my blurb, but I hope it also mentions my degrees in criminal justice. I promise I'm qualified, if that's your concern."

Ginny felt herself staring. Had he just said Secret Service? "Oh. No, obviously that's not my call to make. But sorry, what are you doing here? In my office?"

"I wanted to make sure you're okay, after last night. An event like that can shake a person up. I should also apologize for startling you."

A deep sigh welled up in Ginny's chest. She released it slowly, uncertain how to respond to the man in front of her. He seemed kind enough, and it was a thoughtful gesture to check on her, but she couldn't shake the memory of surprise in his eyes when he'd touched her ruined skin. It brought forth an ache she thought she'd buried long ago.

"I appreciate the gesture, Mr. Tapping, but I have to head out to a very important meeting now and don't really have time to chat."

He nodded and stepped aside as she rose and gathered her things. "Where to?"

Were all Secret Service men so nosy? She immediately scolded herself for the thought. He'd been thoughtful enough to ensure her well-being. She could at least engage in polite conversation. "The Rhoads Museum, just up the road. I'm meeting the curator about a recent request."

"Oh? I haven't been up there yet. Didn't realize it was so close." She glanced sideways at him and he shrugged. "I know, I should visit. Haven't seen much of the town yet, to be quite honest. Maybe I'll hit the museum tomorrow. It isn't like I have any classes to teach this week."

Had no one taken him on a tour of the area? She suddenly felt bad for trying to brush him off. She recalled feeling disconnected and a little lost during her first semester here, and she'd had several months to acclimatize back then. How callous would she be not to offer what help she could? "What are you up to this morning? I can't promise a ride back, but I can give you a lift to the museum since I'm going already."

"That's very kind of you. Are you sure it's no trouble? I do have my own car."

"None at all, especially if you've not visited it yet. It's a small museum but very well curated. I can point out a few local landmarks between here and there, as well."

"In that case, lead the way."

He walked alongside her as she left the Daviau Center, the building that housed her department, and headed toward her car. Ginny noticed that he didn't walk looking forward as most people tended to—the rest of the way to the car and even on the drive, his visual orientation shifted constantly. Overcome by curiosity, Ginny couldn't help but ask, "What are you doing? Can't you sit still?"

Colin's sharp laugh startled her. "Force of habit. Guess you can take the man out of the Secret Service, but not vice versa."

"Why'd you leave?"

He grew silent and Ginny wondered if she'd pried too deep. When he spoke, his words were clipped. "Made a mistake, got dismissed. The inquiry is ongoing."

Ginny mouthed a silent "oh." What could she say to that? Her curious nature tugged on her to ask for more details, but his rigid posture suggested he wasn't comfortable with the topic.

As they trotted up the gray, hewn stone steps of the museum, Ginny realized she'd joined Colin in scanning their surroundings. After giving her statement to the police last night,

they'd told her to be on the lookout for anything unusual in the days ahead, suggesting
that she use the campus Foot Patrol service
in the evenings. The advice was practical, but
useless. The attack had happened indoors in
a building that should have been empty aside
from several staff members, not while she
wandered alone in a public area or parking
lot in the dark.

And the police seemed to have no idea who'd
done it or why. Each time she'd turned another
corner since last night, she couldn't help but
wonder—what if she was walking into another
attack?

"What are you here for, may I ask?" Colin
pushed open the museum doors, glancing behind them at the parking lot for a moment before heading inside. Ginny appeared to be
considering his question, a tiny smile appearing at the corner of her mouth. When she met
his eyes, they sparkled with a contained excitement. When she spoke, her words were clear
and strong. She sounded nothing like the def-
erential woman he'd spoken with so far today.

"If this goes the way I hope it will, I'll obtain the resources I need to potentially pinpoint
an ancient historical site that archaeologists
and historians have been seeking for years."

"Sounds exciting."

She lowered her voice, flicking an apologetic glance toward the staff at the entrance. "If it works out and I find it, or at least find enough information to support my theory on the location, I'll be one step ahead of the other tenure-track candidate at the college. If not, well, I'll be back at square one with this career and have to start all over again at another school. If I can even find another position. It's not like colleges these days are lining up in droves to hire in the humanities."

He kept stride alongside her as she made her way to the curator's office. "Starting over's not always a bad thing. In the Service, I moved through a variety of departments and had to start at the bottom each time." He stopped walking, looked back over his shoulder and then at her. "And now, of course. Can't say I anticipated this career change. Is this where your meeting will be?"

Ginny nodded and raised an eyebrow. "Expecting someone?"

He rubbed his jawline. "After last night, can't be too careful is all. Looks like your contact is here. Thanks again for the ride." He backed up toward a wall of Renaissance paintings as Ginny turned toward a man exiting from the office.

"Professor Anderson?"

Ginny shook the curator's hand as Colin did his best to appear unobtrusive in the moment. They were engaging in the typical social pleasantries and Colin knew this was his cue to move along, but a nagging in the back of his mind stopped him. He didn't feel comfortable leaving Miss Anderson by herself, not after the events of last night and what he'd learned this morning.

After a visit to the local police station, he'd learned that the stun grenade tossed inside the library last night had been military issue. It was privileged information, sure, but a few officers on the local force had recognized him as a former Secret Service agent from news reports several years back and had opened up after he'd asked them a few carefully worded questions. Something about the situation didn't sit right. Nothing in the library had been taken, according to the police. An unprovoked attack on the head librarian and a stun grenade inside a college library held little logic and it worried him.

In fact, crossing the wide-open space of the parking lot to the museum had reminded him just how exposed and vulnerable Ginny Anderson was. Sure, the police didn't know whom the assailant had actually targeted last night, but he didn't like not knowing for certain whether the danger to her had passed. Assuming it had could be a terrible mistake, the kind of mistake he knew all about. The kind of mistake that cost other people their lives.

No, it would be a bad idea to leave Ginny on her own. Touring the museum took an easy second place to making sure the lovely professor wasn't still in serious danger.

THREE

"Your grandchildren are truly adorable," Ginny commented as the curator closed his wallet and slipped it back into his pocket. The man had been eager to show off photos of his family after she'd politely inquired after their well-being. He was such a kind man who obviously cared about others and his work that she'd been happy to listen before turning their meeting's focus onto the real reason she'd come to the museum this morning. "I must say, Mr. Wehbe, thank you so much for meeting with me and considering my request. I really do appreciate it."

"No thanks needed, I'm quite happy to do so. It's not every day that I meet another local academic interested in ancient history and language. Your predecessor spent precious little time with us here, so I was pleased to oblige."

Ginny's hopes skyrocketed. "*Was* pleased to

oblige? I don't suppose that means you already sent in the request?"

Mr. Wehbe chuckled and waved at something—or someone—in his office. "Like I said, it's not every day that someone requests that our little museum borrow tablets from the basement of the Ashmore Museum in Oxford, England. Fortunately, as you are no doubt already aware, I'm still on excellent terms with the curator there and visit my former place of employment several times a year. In fact, only last week I was there for a brief conference."

As Mr. Wehbe spoke, movement at the edge of her vision distracted Ginny from the curator's words. Colin Tapping stood only a few feet away from where she'd left him, gazing at a reproduction of the *Wedding at Cana* late-Renaissance painting.

Surprise and confusion flared in Ginny's senses. Was he eavesdropping on her conversation? She shook her head to dislodge the thought. Maybe he really did have an interest in the artwork. Who was she to think otherwise when she'd just met the man yesterday?

"Professor? Is everything all right?" Mr. Wehbe regarded Ginny with concern.

"Sorry, sorry." Ginny snapped back to reality. "No doubt you heard about the disturbance on campus at the library last night. I spent most of my evening in the hospital and giving a statement to police, and I'm still a little stunned, I suppose."

"Oh! I read about it in the paper this morning but somehow I didn't make the connection. I'm so sorry to hear you were involved. I do hope you take some time to recover. I'm surprised you're here this morning."

"I'm fine," Ginny said, waving his concern off with a pinched smile. After all, she'd truthfully been through much worse in the car accident twenty years ago. "But you were saying?"

"Ah, yes. I'm saying I have the tablets here. I received clearance and was able to bring over the tablets you requested. There is, however, a caveat."

Ginny gaped at the curator. "They're here? Right now? And I can study them immediately?"

"Well, yes and no."

From the curator's office, a gentleman emerged wearing a well-fitted brown tweed suit and Panama hat and carrying a hefty brown leather satchel. He appeared to be at most in his midforties or early fifties. He strode forward and offered his hand to Ginny as Mr. Wehbe made the introductions.

"Professor Anderson, please meet Dr. Hilden. Hilden, this is the ancient history and language professor I've been telling you about. She's the one working on a theory concerning the location of King Ramesh's summer palace in the Kingdom of Amar."

Dr. Hilden smiled warmly and took Ginny's outstretched hand in a firm handshake while she continued to gape at the both of them, struggling to make sense of the moment. Dr. Hilden? The name sounded vaguely familiar. "Pleased to meet you, Professor Anderson."

The curator cleared his throat before continuing, a nervous quaver in his voice. "I wanted to be able to clear this with you ahead of time, but Dr. Hilden is here in an official capacity from the University of Amar. He'll be functioning as a consultant on your work at the request of both the Ashmore Museum and the Amar government. The Amarans were hesitant to approve the request to move the tablets from their safety at Ashmore in England to our little museum in Pennsylvania, but we were able to reach an agreement. Dr. Hilden is a specialist in Amaran history, much like you, but—"

"Less linguistic background." Dr. Hilden tapped on the brown bag he carried. "I have clearance to hand these select tablets to you so long as they don't leave the vicinity of the museum or the college at any time. We'll have you sign a few documents before you head out with them, but ultimately you and I will share responsibility for their safety."

Ginny couldn't believe it, for several reasons. As delighted as she was that she'd received approval to study these ancient tablets so quickly, it felt a bit insulting that the Amarans thought she needed a babysitter to care for their precious artifacts. How many papers had she written on Amaran history and language already? She was well-known among her peers for her work in this area. She had nothing but the utmost respect for Amar's history, and was in fact trying to enrich it with her discovery. But from the sound of things, if she tried to argue her point, Dr. Hilden would be back on an airplane and she'd lose the chance to see the tablets forever, save traveling to the Ashmore Museum in England or the University of Amar. A part-time professor's salary didn't exactly allow her extravagances such as jetting off to another country on a moment's notice.

"Dr. Hilden happened to be at the conference at the Ashmore, as well," said Mr. Wehbe. "Quite a coincidence, yes? Anyhow, Professor Anderson, I imagine you'd like to get started as soon as possible."

Contact information was exchanged and Ginny signed what seemed like a novel's length of documents declaring her responsibility for the artifacts on foreign soil, and she set a meeting with Dr. Hilden for later that afternoon. When the dust from the whirlwind surprise finally began to settle, Ginny found herself standing outside the curator's office with a satchel full of ancient tablets in hand.

She took two steps forward, prying her attention from the bag, only to discover Colin Tapping stood directly in front of her, arms folded across his chest.

And this time, he did not look pleased.

"Productive meeting, I assume?" He approached her, nodding at the heavy leather satchel slung over her shoulder.

She frowned at him. "You can't be finished seeing the museum already. Were you eavesdropping on me?" Her eyebrows pinched together as she tried to step around him.

He fell into step beside her. "No, but I do owe you an explanation."

She stopped and looked him up and down. "You didn't come here to see the art at all, did you, Professor Tapping." Her tone turned flat, making her question a statement.

"I did, honest. And please, stick with Colin. I don't think I'll ever get used to the professor title." He held the door open so she could pass through. She'd hoisted up the satchel and clutched it tight to her chest. "But as we arrived, it dawned on me that you may still be in danger. The police aren't sure where the stun grenade that was thrown last night came from, but the fact that somebody had access to one and used it with possible intent to harm is disconcerting. I hoped you'd allow me to keep an eye out for you on your way back to the campus."

Ginny didn't look at him as she carefully traversed the museum steps, gripping the handrail for balance. "The police I spoke to last night suggested Donna may have fainted and hit her head, before the grenade thing. She'll be in the hospital for a few days to have her condition monitored, but it could have been much worse. I thank God it wasn't."

"Agreed. But it doesn't explain where the grenade came from."

She stopped at the base of the steps, then turned to face him. "I appreciate your concern, but I don't feel like I'm in danger. This isn't an area of town where many exciting things happen, you know?"

Colin paused his ongoing visual scan of the museum grounds and nearby parking lot to focus on the woman standing in front of him. He felt a tug in his chest, part of an ingrained need to protect someone who might be in danger. Twelve years of doing that in various capacities in the Service didn't simply vanish with the change of position.

"I'm glad to hear that. I also know it's true that getting hit by a stun grenade can be mentally and physically traumatizing, despite its less-than-lethal status. I know you've said you don't feel like you're in danger, but I've also noticed you looking over your shoulder."

Ginny shifted her weight and trained her gaze on the sidewalk. "It's silly, right? It was probably a prank, and now I can't help but feel like I'm being watched. I keep hearing the metallic clink of that thing hitting the wall, rolling toward us…" She broke off, eyes unfocused.

Colin knew that look. She'd retreated into herself, reliving the moment. "Ginny. Professor Anderson." He touched her shoulder and her eyes came back into focus, angry at first, then softening as he took his hand away. Her expression, so familiar from last night, reminded him of when he'd accidentally brushed the bumpy red scarring on her cheek. He couldn't see it now—she'd pulled some of her hair up into a messy bun and left the rest to frame her face.

"It's going to be all right." He tried to smile to put her at ease, but the gesture felt tight and insincere. "I won't lie to you, though. I do worry that you might be in danger and I'd like to look out for you, since I have the training and ability to do so. At least until the police have more information on what happened last night."

She shook her head. "I don't need another babysitter."

"Another? Well, I'm not suggesting you do. It makes me nervous that we may have an individual on or around campus with access to serious weaponry, though."

Ginny scoffed and stepped away from him, continuing her journey toward the parking lot and her car. "I think you're blowing this out of proportion. We don't have all the facts and you're acting like there's some big scheme at play to hurt me. Need I remind you that the librarian is the one in the hospital, not me?"

"Under constant surveillance from hospital staff. It's not my intention to cause unnecessary stress, but I want to be up-front with you about my concerns."

She pressed her lips together, then sighed. "I'm only going from here to my office for now. I teach a class later today and I have a meeting with a historical consultant from the Kingdom of Amar. Then I'll probably go to the library if it's reopened, and head home. That's it. Everywhere will be public, and I'll bring a Foot Patrol student along if I need to go anywhere after dark or into any locked-up areas. Does that sound safe enough?"

Under normal circumstances, yes, but if his time in the Secret Service's Presidential Protection Division had taught him anything, it was that threats tended to lurk where the average person least expected them.

"Not particularly. At least let me see you back to campus safely." He noticed she'd begun straining under the weight of the large satchel in her arms. "Can I carry that bag to your car for you?"

She shook her head and tightened her grip around it. "That's the first sensible thing you've said in the past few minutes, but no. I can't allow you to carry it. I'm under agreement with the museum that I will not allow the bag to leave my person unless it's locked up safely in my department's archaeology lab. And it can't go beyond the grounds of the museum or college. It's kind of you to offer, though."

"What's so important about the bag?" A growing frustration at her lack of urgency took over and he flicked two fingers against the bag's handles. He realized his mistake the moment his fingers made contact. Ginny glared at him and it occurred to him that he'd just done the same thing to her that she'd done to him—dismissed her expertise about handling her chosen profession. "Ginny, I'm sorry, I didn't mean to—"

"Have a lovely day, Mr. Tapping. I assume you can find your way back to campus."

He watched as she headed toward her car, her steps sure and confident. He'd handled that in all the wrong ways, and she was under no obligation to accept his offer to look out for her. It was never easy to protect someone who didn't want protecting. He'd have to make a compromise here and keep an eye on her from a distance for today. As soon as she was safely inside her car, he'd run back to the college— he could use the opportunity to scope out potential threat areas, anyway—and rejoin her in her office to try apologizing again.

The woman had to be feeling bruised and battered after last night, so he couldn't blame her for becoming irritated by his assertions. Clearly whatever she had inside that satchel held enough importance for her to ignore the pain, get out of bed and haul herself down to the museum.

Colin continued to scan the area until Ginny reached her car at the edge of the parking lot. He began to relax as she made her way to the passenger side of the little blue hatchback—to secure the heavy bag on the seat beside her, he guessed—but the loud roar of an engine springing to life somewhere nearby sent him back into alert mode.

And then he saw it. A white cube van sped down the parking lot aisle, right toward Ginny.

FOUR

Colin's stomach lurched, first out of concern for how fast the driver was going in a parking lot, and then a second time when he grew sure the van wasn't headed toward an exit. It sped toward Ginny, who had her back to the parking lot as she secured her bags in the car.

Colin didn't waste time asking why or how or whether his suspicion even made sense. He sprang toward her with a burst of speed, grateful he'd kept up his physical training despite being out of the Service these past few years. If only he had his sidearm on hand, he'd have the van incapacitated in seconds without breaking a sweat. Short sprints and lightning-fast reaction times made all the difference when on protective detail.

It took a fraction of a second for Colin to recognize that he was too far away to reach her in time. He kept sprinting as the cube van pulled alongside her. The side door slid open and a man with a black hood pulled low over his face jumped out of the van and grabbed Ginny's waist from behind.

Colin shouted a split second before Ginny's scream rent the air. The man pulled her out of the car and covered her mouth, but her hands remained latched to the ceiling grab handle above the door. *Smart woman*, Colin thought. Her quick reaction would buy him enough time to reach her.

Except that when he drew within several yards of the van, a second hooded assailant jumped out. He pointed a gun in Colin's direction, but Colin was too close and the man's reaction time too slow. Colin ducked as he approached, hoping that the hoodlum didn't have the foresight to fire. He grabbed the gunman's wrist, then yanked it in toward his chest and twisted, forcing the gun down and out of the man's hand. The gun clattered to the ground as Colin used the force of an upper-elbow blow to send the man reeling backward, clutching his jaw.

He risked a glance at Ginny, who—on seeing Colin's approach—had released her grip on the car and twisted around in her attacker's grasp to claw at the man's face. The man now had her wrists locked in his meaty hands as Ginny attempted to kick at him anywhere she could reach.

Colin heard shouts from inside the van—there were more of these guys inside?—but he couldn't afford for it to split his focus further. He kicked the gun on the ground toward a row of parked cars and in two strides had gripped the man attacking Ginny by the neck. He wrenched the attacker away from her, throwing him to the ground with practiced efficiency.

The man rolled as he dropped, leaped to his feet and shouted at his companion to retreat. Both assailants scrambled back inside the van, sliding the door closed as it peeled out of the parking lot, tires squealing.

Colin whirled around to make sure Ginny was all right, but she already leaned against the car with her phone in her hand. "Calling 911?"

She nodded as the operator picked up. With exceptional calm, she told them exactly what had happened and hung up. "Police will be here soon."

He noticed that she too breathed heavily from the exertion moments ago. He was in shape, sure, but an encounter like that took the wind out of anyone, and they were both having trouble catching their breath.

"Are you hurt? Let's get you sitting down

inside the car, all right? Get a few minutes of rest before the emergency teams arrive."

"I'm okay," she said, the calm facade slipping as the adrenaline of the moment faded. "Oh, wow. I can't believe that just happened."

Colin reached into the passenger side of the car, unhooked the bag she'd been carrying and placed it on the driver's seat. She didn't protest as he guided her to sit inside the car, her tremble growing to a full-body shake as the seconds passed. She regarded him with wide, frightened eyes. "Take deep breaths, Ginny. This will pass, but what I need you to do right now is visualize everything that happened. Grab on to details, any small details that you can. Anything at all will help the police find and catch them, got it? I know you want to forget, but the more you can capture in your memory right after this incident, the more accurately you'll be able to tell them what happened."

She nodded, swallowing hard before leaning back against the beige car seat. "Guess I should have taken the day off after all."

"Better to have this happen here than at your home, though."

She sat up in surprise. "At home? You don't think this was random? I guess not, considering."

Colin glanced around the area, staying

watchful in case the van had circled around and come back. He didn't see anything aside from a few startled museum visitors who'd likely witnessed the incident. The familiar wail of emergency sirens rose in the distance. "I think we can rule out random at this point." His gaze was drawn to the bag she'd been carrying. "I'd say now is a better time than ever to finish the conversation we started earlier. What's in the bag?"

Ginny laughed without humor. "Nothing worth kidnapping over, that's for sure. They're a bunch of old clay tablets from one of the Kingdom of Amar's archaeological sites. They've been sitting in the basement of a museum in England for decades, waiting to be translated. It's part of a project I've been working on for a while. I'm planning to decipher them in hopes that they reveal some more information about the location of the summer palace of King Ramesh."

Kidnapping and ancient tablets? It sounded more like a movie than real life. "Is there, I don't know, treasure there?"

Ginny rolled her eyes. "It's not like that at all. Anyone with a modicum of interest in this stuff knows that all the ancient historical sites were looted centuries ago, and many of them were actually looted in ancient times. The more important thing is the location of the summer palace and proving that it actually exists. It's been a point of contention because it would prove the royal lineage of the Amaran desert people. It's a discovery that could change Amar's accepted history and view of their society for the better. It would be a massive find for history, archaeology and the Kingdom of Amar—but nothing worth kidnapping over. There's no financial gain in these tablets themselves, even translated. And selling them untranslated is worth nothing."

"Would *they* know that?"

"That's kind of an important detail if you're kidnapping someone, isn't it? You think some bad guys would kidnap me for a bag full of old, dried clay? If they were gold statues or even Egyptian faience figurines, it'd be another story. Plus, it doesn't explain the grenade last night. I didn't even know I would have these in my possession until about an hour ago."

Colin had to agree with her, but they'd need to talk about it later. An ambulance arrived along with several police cars. Even if Ginny didn't know why she'd been targeted, Colin felt sure of one thing—the woman was in danger, and he might be the only one with the necessary ability to protect her.

Ginny's hands shook as she sprinkled fish food into Tigris's tank. Her little orange-and-blue betta fish swam upward and eagerly picked out pieces of dried shrimp as Ginny put the container away. She clasped her hands, trying to still their tremor.

"You need anything?" Colin leaned against the door frame, standing half in her office and half in the department's main thoroughfare. She appreciated his thoughtfulness in driving her car back to the college and seeing her safely back to the Daviau Center, but for whatever reason, he hadn't left her alone yet. It had started to feel a bit stifling. They were still strangers, after all.

"You don't need to hang around," she said, hoping he'd take the hint. "I know you probably have other things to do."

"We're both off from teaching classes for the week, Professor. We should both be at our respective homes, getting some rest."

"I'm not stopping you."

He grunted and folded his arms. "I don't like the idea of leaving you vulnerable. Two attacks in less than twenty-four hours. That's no prank."

"There's also no proof they're related," Ginny muttered, slumping into her desk chair. She took a deep, slow breath to shove away the wave of anxiety hovering around the edge of her consciousness. "And last I checked, you're not Secret Service anymore, so I'm not obligated to accept any kind of protection from you. I don't appreciate the insinuation that I can't handle myself." She paused, the words catching in her throat because she *had* needed him there. If Colin hadn't been present last night or this morning, she'd be having a very different conversation. Possibly with an abductor. Or a nurse.

Colin grunted again and stared out into the departmental office. "Never said you're not capable. Everyone needs help sometimes, and while you're right—you're not obligated—I'd consider myself responsible if anything happened to you that was in my power to prevent."

Ginny breathed deeply as she watched Tigris swim laps in his wide, plastic fishbowl. She did appreciate Colin's help. He'd come to her rescue without hesitation, the kind of attractive and strong hero whom plenty of girls would love to be saved by, but he'd already told her it came down to instinctive response born through training. Not because he had any kind of personal investment in her well-being.

Of course, she should have expected that from someone who'd seen her scar.

"I'll think about it, Colin." With her heart finally beating at a more normal pace, Ginny picked up the satchel of tablets and set them on her desk. Even the events of today couldn't dislodge the excitement of physically having in her hands a set of ancient tablets she'd only dreamed of seeing. Anxiety followed close behind, too—at best, she'd thought that Mr. Wehbe might find someone to dig the tablets out of crates in the Ashmore Museum's basement where they'd spent the past sixty or so years, then take updated photos and send those over. But to have entrusted her with the physical objects?

They were valuable from a historical point of view. Potential evidence to support her theory. But while the knowledge that might be gained from them was priceless, the tablets themselves were not. No one would try to abduct her over a bunch of old tablets.

She picked up a sand-colored oblong tablet about the width and length of two candy bars, then ran her fingers lightly over the inscription. The surface felt rough and grainy, though environmental factors had smoothed some of its edges.

"Not much to look at, is it?" Colin regarded

the object she held with cool detachment. "Wonder if the original tablets with the Ten Commandments looked anything like that?"

Ginny smiled to herself, used to these kinds of questions. "Actually, those tablets—"

"Professor Anderson?" A voice from the hallway was followed by a face peering around the corner of her office door. Colin stepped aside to allow Sam, a teaching assistant for her Introduction to Near Eastern Studies class, inside. The student was covering the front reception desk for Mrs. McCall, the departmental secretary, who'd stayed home this morning to nurse her sick toddler.

He waved a large, flat yellow mailing envelope in his hand. "I meant to catch you when you came back, but this arrived for you a half hour or so ago. Right before you got back from the museum."

"Thanks, Sam." She took it and frowned at the front. The envelope was nondescript, completely unremarkable, with no stamp or return address. Only her name had been affixed to the envelope with a printed label, neglecting to mention her box number or even the name of her department. It had obviously not been through the mail system but simply left here for her. "Who dropped this off?"

Sam shrugged. "A phone call came in from

an alumnus and I had to check the filing cabinet for some old records. When I turned around it was there on the desk, no one around. I'm sure it wasn't there before. Weird, huh?"

"Probably another interdepartmental memo or something." She glanced at Colin, who also shrugged. She slipped a finger underneath the envelope flap and ripped it open. Inside rested several sheets of paper, which she slipped out with care. A letter? Who wrote a letter these days when they could write an email? It looked as though it had been composed on an old-fashioned typewriter, the inked letters leaving a slight indentation on the paper's surface.

She began reading. Her stomach dropped.

Dear Professor Anderson,

Greetings. I do hope this letter finds you well, and I must ask you to please excuse the nature by which I have delivered this correspondence. Circumstances beget such a necessity and besides, I abhor technology in all its forms, avoiding it at all costs—insofar as it is reasonable to do so. First, however, I must apologize for the rude actions of my compatriots earlier this morning. Please be assured that they acted out of turn in assaulting your per-

sonage, and it will not happen again so long as our interactions warrant it thusly.

Ginny waved a hand at Colin, her eyes glued to the page. In an instant, he was by her side, reading the letter over her shoulder.

I am truly grateful that a gentleman was present to thwart those characters who I assure you misunderstood the nature of my instructions. They were in no way directed to approach you in such an invasive manner. It is not...diplomatic, shall we say.

But now we come to the real issue, yes? The tablets you have in your possession. I am aware of their presence and I am aware of their importance. However, it may behoove you to know that the work you do is not so innocent as the academic world would have you believe. Allow me to make you an offer, Professor. Fifty thousand dollars in exchange for your assurance that you will abandon this research project.

You will place all of your existing notes and theorems inside this envelope. Drop it in the waste bin outside the public area commonly referred to as the "quad" at four o'clock this afternoon. Destroy any remaining files that contain your work and return the tablets to the museum. Explain that you have discovered your theories are no longer feasible with the available evidence and that you will be publishing a retraction of your preliminary reports. Yes, Professor Anderson, I have read your preliminary reports on the summer palace location. A little far-fetched, hmm?

Once you have completed these tasks, you will discover yourself fifty thousand dollars richer. I imagine this will go a long way on a part-time professor's salary.

Remember, four o'clock today. I advise against tardiness in this matter.

The letter ended there. No signature and nothing on the other side of the page.

Ginny's hand shook, blurring the words. She had so many questions, she couldn't keep track of them all. Was this some kind of a joke? A student thinking it would be funny to mess with her head after what had happened this morning?

Surely no one would be so dense as to believe that she'd give up her research—her potentially career-changing research—for a bribe.

Colin reached across and plucked the paper from her trembling hands, and a sense of relief that he was there rushed through her. He'd know what to do, wouldn't he?

"Well, that's odd. Looks like this was typed up manually."

Or maybe not. She plunked her elbows on the desk, covering her face with her hands. "What's going on? I teach ancient history. I don't have secrets or hidden knowledge. It's like I'm stuck in a bad made-for-TV movie."

Colin glanced out into the department common area, then took two steps to cross her tiny office and look out its small window. He pulled across the gauzy curtain so that it hid them from view. "I wish I knew. It's strange that whoever sent this would target you without an explanation. Sounds like someone wants you to stop your research, but based on what you've told me, it doesn't make a whole lot of sense. There's no financial gain, unless someone's reputation is at stake. Is that a possibility?"

Ginny laughed bitterly. "Only my own professional reputation. If I publish a retraction of my earlier work, I'll have set my career back by several years. I won't be eligible for the tenure-track position and my next assertions will be met with severe scrutiny."

"Sounds like you care a lot about what other people think."

"When it comes to my professional reputation and the future of my career? Absolutely."

"Careers aren't the be-all and end-all of life."

"Of course they are—oh." Her face fell when she realized what she'd said. "Sorry. You said you didn't leave the Secret Service by choice?"

"No, and it's fine. I don't talk about it a lot and I'd prefer not to." Ginny started to apologize, to explain that she'd only been curious, but he held up a hand to stop her and tapped on the envelope instead. "I'm going to take this down to the police station. I can't guarantee they'll be able to do a lot since there's no specific threat here, but I'm hoping the admission of responsibility for the events of the past twenty-four hours will be enough to tie it all together."

"What about fingerprints? Tracing the paper or office supplies or ink? I've seen that on television."

"Yours, mine and Sam's. Maybe the sender touched it, but who sends a threatening letter and leaves a fingerprint? For that matter, who sends a physical letter instead of, say, calling?"

Ginny clutched a tablet in one hand and brushed the outside edge before tracing the shapes on the inside. "Someone who doesn't like new things. New technology. If someone is trying to terrorize me into stopping my research, they must have an interest in old things."

"That's one possibility. But the label with your name looks printed off a computer, not a typewriter."

"The sender mentioned associates. Maybe someone did it for him or her?"

As Colin's mouth set into a firm, hard line, Ginny's confidence faltered. If he couldn't figure it out, what chance did she have against this mysterious adversary?

Colin stole a glance at Ginny, not at all surprised by the weariness on her face. He'd seen that look plenty of times on the faces of those he'd protected. Presidents, diplomats, persons of national importance, didn't matter whom. No one had an easy time when it came to threats on his or her life. This wasn't the first threatening letter he'd seen, but it was one of the most carefully put together. Generic envelope, generic paper and an assumption that Ginny would follow through. And the writer had the gall to drop it off in person.

"Are there security cameras around here?" he asked.

She shook her head. "Only at the entrances on either end of the building. The ones you see inside are dummies to deter students from destructive behavior. You could ask for security footage from outside, but it won't be easy to go through. There'll be a few hundred students coming and going, since some of the school's administration offices are upstairs."

It'd be a start, at least. The police would want to have a look at the footage as soon as he told them about the letter, but he wanted to get a look at it first. He pulled his phone out of his pocket to dial the security office. "I'm going to make a quick call and stand right outside your door, all right?" He watched as Ginny nervously rubbed her fingers over a tablet, her shoulders high and tense. "Should you be touching those things like that? I thought ancient stuff needed gloves and a secure environment."

Some of the tension in her shoulders dropped. Good. The woman needed a few moments to relax, to rebuild her strength. Just in case.

Just in case. He hated the necessity of thinking that way, but better to be prepared than caught unawares. Those kinds of mistakes could be fatal—and one had been for the woman he was assigned to protect two years ago. Lynn Gustav, daughter of a diplomat, had stolen his heart and his focus. He'd been distracted in a critical moment and an assassin's bullet found its mark. He hadn't been able to save her.

He would not let his guard down like that again.

"Some ancient things, yes," she was saying. "But not everything, otherwise only a few people would be able to study them. Clay tablets are durable, as long as you don't throw them on the ground or run them over with a tractor. They've lasted this long, after all."

Colin reached across to touch one, wondering at the texture of a thousands-of-years-old piece of clay, but Ginny yanked the one she held out of reach.

"Sorry." Her face flushed. "I'm the only one allowed to touch them, remember? Aside from Mr. Wehbe and the Amaran representative overseeing my project. The tablets are durable and not financially worth much, but they're still valuable pieces of history in other ways. And they don't belong to the United States. Our agreement is that their handling is to be strictly controlled."

"Ah, yes. Protocol. Who knew pieces of clay

had protocol?" Much to Colin's surprise, he couldn't take his eyes off her reddened cheeks. She combed more strands of blond hair over her scarred cheek, fingers moving absently— as if it had become a habit she wasn't even aware of.

His phone began to buzz, reminding him that he'd been about to make a phone call to campus security. He frowned at the caller ID. Private number?

"Tapping," he answered.

"Good afternoon, Professor. Is that what they're calling you these days? Must be quite the change."

Colin swallowed a burst of disbelief. "Sir?"

A chuckle on the other end confirmed the identity of the caller. "And hello to you as well, Tapping. Surprised to hear from me?"

Of course he was. He hadn't directly spoken to anyone from the Secret Service since the day they'd completed his discharge papers, the director having bowed to political pressure to dismiss him the day after the incident. The diplomat whose daughter had been killed had called for blood, and what easier resolution than to fire the agent who'd failed to protect her? It had only been his career ended as a result, taking the heat off the Secret Service. Not that he didn't blame himself for what had happened. He'd known from the beginning that it was unwise to become romantically involved with a protectee and had fallen for her anyway.

"Deputy Director Bennett. I'm not sure if I should say it's good to hear from you or not."

"Fair enough. How're things? Got a good gig up there?"

Colin grimaced and stole another glance at Ginny. She looked up at him quizzically, but he'd have to answer her questions later. As nice as it should be to receive a personal phone call from the Secret Service's deputy director, he had a feeling it wasn't a social call. After all, Deputy Director Bennett had been the one to sign his discharge papers. "Pays the bills."

"Not thrilled to hear my voice, are you? I get it, Tapping. I really do."

"Deputy Director, I'm in the middle of something at the moment. Is there something pressing?"

"Down to business. You haven't changed a bit." Bennett's voice softened. "You were a good agent, Colin. I'm still sorry things ended the way they did."

"Part of the job, Deputy Director. Consequences for every action."

"Yes, but…ah, well. Speaking of people needing protection."

"Very subtle."

"I do my best. Listen, Tapping, we've been hearing rumblings about some shakeups happening overseas that may tie into a little drama unfolding in your corner. I realize this is unconventional, but we've been requested to keep our eyes open for an Amaran representative en route to Pennsylvania. Heading to your corner of the state. Know anything about this?"

Colin thought back to Ginny's meeting at the museum this morning. Hadn't she mentioned that she'd met a gentleman who'd arrived from the Kingdom of Amar to assist with her work? "I think he may already be here, sir. Name of Hilden? He's working with a colleague."

"Already there?" The sound of shuffling papers reached Colin's ears before Bennett's voice came through the receiver again. "That's what we get for receiving information secondhand. Look, we weren't asked to specifically provide a detail for him, but the incident with the military-issue grenade on your campus and this Dr. Hilden's proximity has the White House a little nervous. We're on good terms with the kingdom, but you know how quickly things change in the world these days."

Colin ground his teeth as Deputy Director Bennett talked. Two years ago, he'd have jumped all over this kind of information, but right now it did nothing but frustrate him, reminding him of what he no longer had. "I'm not sure what I have to do with this."

Bennett sighed. "I know you owe us nothing, Colin. And I know helping us out is the last thing you probably want to do, after what happened. But our hands are full over here dealing with a number of sensitive political situations, and we can't spare a man for a detail that's not a sure thing or specifically requested by the president. The local police chief I talked to mentioned that you were up at the college there."

"Let me guess, you want me to keep an eye on this Dr. Hilden character. Make sure no one lobs a live one in his direction, is that it?"

"More or less. Off the record. Informal. Just keep an eye out. As a favor."

"What makes you think I'd have any interest in doing you a favor?" Colin tried to swallow down his anger, but it rose fast and furious. "Not that it makes any difference to you, but I've got someone else I'm watching out for at the moment. Another professor here is working on some ancient tablets on loan from the Kingdom of Amar and she's been the target of…look, you know what? Never mind. Have a good day, Deputy Director."

Colin hung up and thumped his head against the door frame. Two years had changed him, whether Bennett saw it or not. He'd never have talked out of turn and hung up like that two years ago. Bennett didn't deserve it, as it wasn't entirely the man's fault that Colin had been dismissed from the Secret Service.

Bennett hadn't been the one who failed to protect his assignment. Lynn Gustav had died on Colin's watch, no one else's. If only he hadn't let his heart get so involved. If only he hadn't taken her safety for granted, allowing himself to be distracted by his feelings.

"Who was that?" Wide-eyed, Ginny flicked her chin at the phone. "Didn't sound good." She bent to replace the tablet she'd been holding inside the leather satchel.

A sense of determination rose up from within, combining with his finely honed instinct from years of training. Active agent or not, it was his duty to protect critical individuals from potential danger by any means necessary. With a growl of frustration, he ignored Ginny's inquiry and hit Redial. Bennett picked up on the first ring.

"I've got a better idea," Colin said before the man could speak. "The colleague here working on ancient tablets from Amar is the one who's being targeted, not Hilden. I truly believe she's the one in danger, and it's her and those tablets you need to be worried about. Since she's the one being targeted, she's my priority. Her and these foreign artifacts. That said, I'll keep an eye out for any danger facing Hilden and an ear to the ground, just in case. If I hear anything unusual, I'll report in if and when I have any information. But I'm going to need something in return."

Colin heard Deputy Director Bennett drum his fingers on his desk. "You do us a favor, I'll do you a favor. You need resources or backup and we're there. You know the Service takes care of its own, Tapping, active or not. So long as you want to cooperate with us, we'll have your back."

"I still believe in the tenets and values of the Service, Deputy Director. That will never change, and that's why I'm doing this. It's the right thing to do." He refused to allow another woman to come to harm if he had the power to stop it.

"Of course. You're an honorable man and I respect that. And, Tapping?"

The deputy director's tone of voice changed, became more sympathetic. Colin tensed, unsure whether he wanted to continue this conversation. "What is it?"

"I know your dismissal case is still in limbo, tied up in red tape. You've been waiting to hear back for two years on whether it's a permanent cut."

"I'm well aware." Why was Bennett opening this old wound? "I'm not sure how that's relevant."

The deputy director cleared his throat before continuing. "All I'm saying is it would be prudent for your image among the leadership here if this goes well. Maybe even to the point of pushing your case through faster. And with a positive result."

"Are you saying that if I cooperate with you on this, I might get my job back?"

There was a pause on the other end of the line. "I'm saying there's a very good chance we'll see you in uniform again. You were an asset to the Service, Tapping. The kind of man this country needs protecting its president. A good agent."

Colin hung up for a second time and stared at the phone in his hands. "But not good enough."

FIVE

Ginny's heart pounded at seeing the expression on Colin's face. He looked angry, and from the one side of the phone call she'd heard, it appeared an old wound had been reopened.

"I have to go to my meeting," she squeaked, her brain still trying to make sense of his words into the phone. "Do you really think I'm in that much danger? Why not leave it to the police?"

"Secret Service is technically law enforcement, highly specialized in protective measures. That's how I know how to operate, and I will react without hesitation when needed."

"I see." But she didn't, not really. She'd have to trust that he knew what he was talking about. "What about my meeting?"

Colin punched at his phone while motioning for her to gather up her things. "I'm coming with you, but we need to make a stop first."

"I don't think—"

"You've been attacked twice, Professor. Stay close and hopefully there won't be a third time. I'll watch the security footage and brainstorm about this letter drop while you have your meeting. You won't even know I'm there."

Ginny saw the wisdom in his plan, but that didn't mean she had to like it. She waited in silence with Colin as he talked his way into obtaining a digital file of the afternoon's footage outside the Daviau Center from the security office. After they'd picked up a laptop from his office in the Criminology Department, she noticed something odd. Every time she took more than a few steps in front or behind Colin, he cleared his throat. "What are you doing?"

"Remember, I need you within arm's reach," he said, holding open the door to the library. Ginny watched him visually scan the area behind them, then proceeded with him to the meeting room. It was located on the library's main floor only a few steps from the busy circulation desk. Ginny couldn't imagine being accosted here. In the light of day, her memory of last night's grenade attack in this very building felt like the remnants of a dream.

"Do you have to come inside?" Nervousness crept up the back of her throat. She already felt low on confidence at the thought of working with someone else who could likely match or surpass her knowledge of Amaran history. A quick peek into the meeting room showed Dr. Hilden already waiting inside reading a journal article, despite her efforts to arrive fifteen minutes early to set up.

In response, Colin stalked across the floor and returned dragging a small table and chair, which he set up outside the meeting room door. "I'll watch the footage right here. You go in and have your meeting. How long will you be?"

Ginny sighed. She couldn't deny the sense of safety that came over her at having him around, but this babysitter business was already wearing thin. "I don't know. An hour or two?"

He nodded. "Finish before four if you can. I have a feeling that whoever wrote that letter may start getting anxious, and I don't want to be cornered in here if that happens."

Ginny started to retort that even the letter writer had said the attempted abduction this morning had been a mistake—but the words died on her lips when she saw the sincerity in his eyes. Eyes that suddenly seemed just as dangerous as their unknown enemy. A woman could drown in those eyes.

She shook herself out of it and headed inside the room, acutely aware of Colin's presence right outside the door. She could still see his profile as he set up his laptop and began watching the security footage. How on earth had she ended up in this mess?

"Professor Anderson," Dr. Hilden boomed, standing to shake her hand with his firm grip. He placed the journal article on the table and tapped on the top paragraph. "Intriguing assertion you've made here regarding the palace coordinates, I must say. Fascinating preliminary work."

Ginny swallowed her nerves. She was smart, capable. She could do this. "Thank you, but like I said in the thesis, it's only preliminary. Hopefully these tablets will fix that, however."

"Of course, of course." He placed a briefcase on the table and opened it up, pulling additional papers from inside. "My own notes, of course. I'd be honored to read yours as well, as I assume you have plenty more work conducted by now in this area. Perhaps a few responses to the criticisms? Curator Wehbe implied as much."

Ginny steeled her resolve, thinking of the letter and its demands for her to abandon this project and pass off—or destroy—her research. Could it have been the product of a jealous colleague, eager to learn her research to publish it as his or her own? Stranger things had happened in academia. "There's not much, but we can work through what I have. You're the consultant, after all."

For the next two hours, Ginny walked Dr. Hilden through her theories, explaining her current ideas and responding to his criticisms while trying to ignore Colin's occasional glances into the room. Together, she and Dr. Hilden were able to map several preliminary translations of two small tablets, and Ginny was elated to discover that one of them contained a subtle reference to a royal building.

As she packed the tablets back up, her heart pounded double time. The royal building reference had been written using a specific ancient Amaran hieroglyph that she'd been theorizing for a while might refer to the king's summer palace. If that was the case, she'd already come one step closer to confirming the palace's location. To have found anything this soon after beginning work on the tablets went far beyond her wildest expectations.

"Great work this afternoon, Professor Anderson," Dr. Hilden said, inclining his head as he withdrew from the room. "You're quite persistent in your research. I have no doubt you'll find what you're looking for in due time."

"I sure hope so," she murmured. A glance at the clock in the corner of the room made her heart lurch into her throat—it was five minutes to four. The time had passed quickly. Had Colin learned anything useful from the security footage? Bag packed, she stepped out of the room to find Colin also packed up, shaking Dr. Hilden's hand and making introductions.

"Former Secret Service?" Dr. Hilden was saying, looking mildly perturbed. "I see. How unexpected to meet someone of your trained caliber here. If you'll excuse me, I have a scheduled conference call. Good day."

As Dr. Hilden walked away, Colin turned to Ginny and shrugged. "I get all kinds of reactions," he explained. "Sometimes it makes people nervous. I'm used to it by now. We should get going."

The library had quieted at this time of day, with most students still in class or heading to the cafeteria to eat before evening classes began. A student behind the circulation desk waved at her and Ginny waved back, recognizing the student from one of her classes.

"You okay, Professor?"

Had the whole school heard about what happened? "I'm fine, Shelby. It's Donna I'm most concerned about."

Shelby grimaced and bit the corner of her lip. "I heard about that this morning. Some of

the library staff are going to head down and
visit her at the hospital tonight."

"I'm sure she'll appreciate that." Ginny
glanced at the clock, feeling the urge to keep
moving. "Give her a hug from me, all right?"

Shelby nodded as a slow grin spread across
her face. "I will, but you can come too and give
it to her yourself, if you want. Plus, Roger left
another note for her last night. He must have
come in to clean up after the explosion and
heard about what happened. Awfully sweet,
don't you think? I just wish we could set them
up for real."

Ginny smiled at the memory of her last
conversation with Donna. "You and me both,
Shelby."

"We should move," Colin said, touching
the small of her back. She jumped away at his
touch, then felt her cheeks grow warm. He'd
only tried to direct her away from the circulation desk and toward the front door. "I realize this might sound counterintuitive, but we
should head to the quad. You'll need to tell me
where it is, though. I'm not fully familiar with
the campus yet."

Go *to* the place the letter writer wanted
them? "Won't we be walking into a trap?"

"Trust me, please. Location?"

Ginny felt like hoisting her bag and running

in the exact opposite direction. Could she really trust him? He had been kicked out of the Secret Service, after all. Maybe he wasn't as good as he claimed. But what other option did she have? "It's like a square courtyard in the center of the main college buildings. Quadrilateral, so it has four main paths at the edges leading from the different buildings around it. You probably walk through it every day, several times. There's a bench, a bulletin board for student announcements, some light posts and a trash can…"

"Got it. It's a high-traffic area, so that's an interesting choice. Do you have an envelope in your bag? Something similar to what you were instructed to use for the drop?"

Ginny stopped midstride. "Colin, what's going on? What are you going to do?"

He faced her, jaw set in grim determination. "I'm going to make certain that the letter you received wasn't an opportunist's prank, and try to create some evidence for the police."

He couldn't be serious. "I don't understand. Did you find something on the security tape?"

Colin shook his head and Ginny saw, for a split second, a sliver of uncertainty. "Teachers, students, support staff. Nothing obvious. And the footage is grainy. The equipment here is long overdue for an upgrade."

"Which means?"

He locked eyes with her, unwavering. "We're going to try to draw this person out and finish it. Right now."

Colin knew he'd be taking a risk. It might be a terrible idea or the best idea he'd had so far. Either way, he wanted to expose the individual behind these strikes at Ginny before the person could try again.

Experience and training had taught him that people who made demands and threats liked to stick around to see their plans carried through. Whoever sent the letter would be watching her right now, and probably watching the drop point, too. During Ginny's meeting, he'd spoken with the police about the letter over the phone and determined several contingency plans, so there should be several officers stationed around the campus, watching for anything amiss. He'd hand off the letter to them for fingerprint analysis once the four o'clock deadline passed.

But now, Ginny stared at him as though he'd told her they were about to drive a car off a cliff.

"Are you crazy?" She winced and then lowered her voice. "How do you propose to do that? Didn't the letter come from the same person who tried to have me kidnapped?"

It was the first true outburst of emotion he'd seen from her so far, and as much as he tried to suppress it, he was jolted by the realization that she looked quite lovely when fired up. He shook it off, though—such an observation was not relevant to the job at hand.

He chose his words carefully, trying not to cause undue fear at his plan. "We need to try to get ahead of this letter writer. The letter's tone was stern but not violently aggressive." He didn't remind her of the implicit, veiled threat in the final line. "The danger here, according to the sender, is if you don't follow through. I'm no psychologist, but it sounds like this person expects you to follow their orders. So that's what we're going to do."

He reached into his waistband to double-check the security of the SIG Sauer pistol he'd slipped there during their quick visit to his office a few hours ago. He might not technically be Secret Service, but he still had the arsenal and training to take anyone down with a single long-range shot if necessary.

Ginny hoisted her bag to her chest and backed away. "I'm not giving up my research."

Colin sighed and stepped back within arm's reach, lowering his voice. "That's what the false envelope is for. There's a blonde police officer who'll borrow your sweater and purse to make the drop—"

"Uh, that won't work."

Did she have to interrupt him before he'd even finished explaining? "Of course it will. All she needs to do is slip the envelope into the trash bin and leave."

Ginny gestured to her clothes. "And we're changing clothes where? Does she have something in my size? And a fake leather satchel? And does she wear her hair across her face like this?"

Colin didn't miss the pain that rippled across her features with the final question. "We have to work with what we've got."

"But Colin, if the letter writer is really watching, and based on what you've been saying and what's been happening, it seems like whoever is doing this knows what I look like and where I'll be. They've had eyes on me one way or another most of this time. You think a police officer in a disguise is going to fool them? They'll know about the leather satchel with the tablets, and you know I absolutely cannot give them up."

She was right. Colin hated that he couldn't win this one and that it came down to a satchel full of tablets with international regulations.

He gritted his teeth, swallowing down the frustration. "What are you suggesting?"

"I'll do it." Ginny held her head high, straightening her posture. "I'll make the drop."

"No. Absolutely not. We don't know what to expect. I can't let you do that."

"We have to work with what we've got," she said, echoing his words. "And besides, you said it yourself. The real danger here seems to be a threat if I don't follow through."

He had to admit, it made sense. All it required was for her to make a single drop. Maybe twenty feet into the quad and then directly out again. He'd have her covered with the SIG Sauer, and there should be at least four other plainclothes policemen here by now to cover the remaining angles.

He could protect her. But he didn't like it. There was always a "what if?" to consider.

"I'm doing it," she said, before he could protest further. "I trust that you can protect me."

Her words jolted him into action. She trusted him? Maybe not completely—he could still see uncertainty in her eyes—but he wouldn't let her down today, and they were running out of time to make a move. "I'll have you in sight the entire time, but I'll be in cover. There are other officers watching you from other locations. I don't think our perp will make an appearance until after the drop, but the info you're leaving has to be collected one way or another. I'm going to wait them out."

Ginny blanched, though her expression remained resolute. "I'll walk right back to you."

He lifted the hem of his shirt half an inch so she could see the concealed weapon. "I'll have your back. As long as I can see you, I can protect you. My counter-assault training for the Service means I can accurately hit a target with a handgun at fifty yards. We're going to end this, Ginny, so you can get on with your life."

Her slow nod told him she understood. If anything, this maneuver came out of a need Colin saw to fake out and capture either the letter sender or the person sent to pick up her materials *before* whichever one realized the package was a fake. He had every confidence that the letter sender was actually after her research—not Ginny specifically—and doubted he'd have to discharge his weapon today.

Ginny drew the false envelope from her bag as Colin gave her specific instructions on where to walk and how to get back to him without making it obvious. A quick phone call to his police contact confirmed the new plan. At thirty seconds to four, Colin slipped into cover in a small walkway between two campus buildings, crouching behind a bush in its lengthened afternoon shadow. Ginny strode forward with purpose, head held high.

Colin wished he could have done more to reassure her, but that wouldn't be appropriate under the circumstances. She was his protectee, his priority. And besides, every time he accidentally touched her, she flinched as though burned.

He tensed as she approached the trash bin, grateful for the police assistance to keep any wandering students and visitors out of the area—but he did worry that they might not have been discreet enough about it. What would happen if the person they were trying to catch figured out a trap had been set?

In front of the bin, Ginny hesitated. She glanced around, behind and then over at Colin. Then she dropped the envelope in the trash bin. Colin held his breath. Nothing else moved in the quad, save the rustling tree leaves above. He exhaled, mentally urging Ginny back to him. She jogged three steps away from the trash bin before Colin spotted something shiny flying through the air toward the center of the quad, streaks of orange flickering through the air as it made its arc. *A homemade explosive!*

"Get back!" Colin shouted as he burst from his hiding place. The object hit the pavement and exploded, sending shards of glass, cement and burning debris flying through the air. Everything stank like gasoline.

Ginny tumbled forward and hit the earth hard. Colin raced toward her, drawing on instinct and shoving away the terror for Ginny's safety and his sudden, overwhelming sense of failure. He reached her seconds before two of the policemen did, guns drawn.

"You two, watch our backs," he shouted. "Radio the others to get security scouring the area for whoever threw that thing." He crouched to check on Ginny. She'd risen up on her forearms, face down toward the pavement. He didn't see any obvious wounds, but that didn't mean she wasn't hurt. "Ginny. Miss Anderson. Talk to me."

Ginny groaned and pushed herself up farther. She placed a hand to her face and it came away red and sticky. "Oh, no. No, no, no."

"Let me see." Despite her protests, Colin took her chin and checked the extent of the damage. She'd received nasty scrapes on her nose, the apple of her unscarred cheek and her palms. "These will heal up quickly. Surface wounds. I'm more concerned about what that fall did. Can you stand?"

Ginny's eyes had filled with tears and Colin released her chin in surprise. She shook her head, then looked around in alarm. "My bags. The tablets!"

"Right here." Colin reached across to her other side, where they'd fallen. A tiny tongue of fire flickered on the corner of the satchel where a drop of ignited gasoline had landed. Colin smothered it with the edge of his shirt. "They're safe with you. Again, I need you to try standing. We can't stay out here."

With a tearful nod, she allowed him to offer his arm and help her stand. He picked up her bags and she took them from him, despite the wobbliness of her steps. Colin noticed she kept touching the scrape on her cheek, the side she didn't usually hide. "Don't touch that. You'll risk infection."

She pulled her hand away and glanced back at the policemen who now guarded the scene. "What happened?"

"I made an error in judgment. I thought we could get one step ahead. I should never have let you make the drop yourself." He'd thought they could just walk away and wait for someone to retrieve it, then catch the culprit red-handed. But a homemade firebomb? They'd been made. Their opponent must have noticed what they were doing and taken matters into his or her own hands. And they might have succeeded, because he needed to get Ginny away from here and get her checked over, and most of the police were already scouring the campus for the bomber. That meant this trash can, with the dropped materials inside, would be left unattended and the envelope easily retrieved. Even if the contents inside were fake, the letter writer didn't know that and had tried to turn the situation in his or her favor.

Whoever they were dealing with was smart, able to adjust plans and think on the fly. Probably the benefit of having lackeys at one's disposal, which made it even more difficult for Colin to anticipate what would happen next. After a move like this, the likelihood of being able to protect the woman beside him from another attack dropped drastically. "Let's get you out of here." He pointed at the remaining two officers who stood at the edge of the quad. One was on the radio calling for backup. "Don't let this trash bin out of your sight, but stay vigilant. Someone anticipated we'd be here and they're trying to draw us away."

He led Ginny back to the Daviau Center, growing more concerned by the minute as she remained silent. He hadn't seen her head hit the ground, but it might be worthwhile for her to get checked out regardless. Two major falls in two days could do plenty of cumulative damage. "I'm going to call the campus nurse down to check you over once we get to your office, since that's closer than trying to get all the way to the med center. Can you make it to your office?"

"I'm fine," she mumbled. He had a hard time believing that.

In the department's main office, Sam still filled in at the front desk. The student stood in surprise as they entered, but Colin shot him a look that suggested he hold any questions for the time being. They headed toward Ginny's little office and she dug out her key ring, flipping through a slew of keys in many different shapes and sizes. "Do you even know what half of those open?"

"I used to." Ginny placed the correct key in the lock. "It's more about possibility than the known. I like old mysteries."

Her voice had grown stronger since leaving the quad. Good. Colin was just as concerned about these events taking a mental toll as he was about the physical. Before he could stop himself, his eyes were tugged to look at the ruined side of her face that remained covered by a veil of blond hair. Speaking of old mysteries…

He saw a slight frown on Ginny's lips. She'd seen him looking and it bothered her. It wouldn't do to have this tension between them—he needed to have her full trust and confidence if he was going to protect her from additional harm.

"Sorry, Ginny, I—"

"Save it." She swung her office door open and stepped backward with a cry of surprise.

The office had become a disaster zone.

Books and papers were strewn around the small office, her chair overturned and her desk drawers open with their contents spread across the floor. Tigris's bowl lay empty in the middle of the room.

Someone had trashed her office—and that someone had a key.

SIX

Colin didn't waste a second. He raced back to Sam at the front desk. The student had giant, noise-cancelling headphones covering his ears, and his nose was buried in a textbook as he tapped out the rhythm of a song with the end of a bright yellow highlighter. Colin reached over the desk and yanked the headphones off. Sam looked up with a shout of alarm.

"Did anyone come through here this afternoon?" Sam's stunned face caused Colin's already mounting frustration to rise further. "Anyone? I'm waiting."

"Sure," Sam sputtered. "Tons of people. Students coming to pick up assignments, and there are offices of a bunch of teachers here. I mean, I don't know what you want me to say."

"Who came through here who would have a key to Professor Anderson's office?"

The student's face scrunched up in confusion. "Professor Anderson's office? She has the key. The custodial staff has a master key, but the only other key is right here." He tapped on a desk drawer beside him. "I have them while I'm covering for Mrs. McCall. Why?"

"My office has been broken into, Sam." Ginny joined Colin at the desk, weariness etched across her face. Her shoulder sagged from the weight of the tablet satchel. If only she'd let him help her carry it—but no, that wasn't her call to make.

Sam's eyes widened, his mouth opening and closing like Ginny's poor little betta fish. "But that's impossible. I didn't see anyone, and I'm the only other person here."

"Open the drawer, Sam." Colin tried to keep the growl out of his voice, but the kid's hesitance told him that perhaps Sam wasn't the best fill-in for the regular receptionist after all. "Ginny, you're exhausted. Go sit down."

Sam shook his head. "I'm telling you, I've been here the whole time and the keys are right—" He pulled open the drawer, reached inside, and pulled out...nothing. Surprise and panic rippled across the student's features as he scraped around inside the drawer. Still finding nothing, he repeated the process with the rest of the desk drawers, coming up empty-handed. "I don't understand."

Next to Colin, Ginny sighed. It didn't look

as if she planned to relax anytime soon. "Sam? You're sure you were here the whole time?"

Sam's expression turned sheepish. "Yes?"

"Try again," Colin said, not bothering to hide the growl this time. "The truth."

Sam moaned and thumped his head onto the desk. "My girlfriend came in like, ten minutes ago. She needed help getting a bag of chips unstuck from the vending machine. I was only gone for like, two minutes, I promise."

"And that was enough time for the keys to get stolen, a professor's office to get broken into and the place trashed. Now someone out there has the keys to this entire department and probably the building. Am I right?"

Sam's upper body remained prone against the desk.

"Finish out the day, Sam," Ginny said, her voice tense. "I'll be letting the department head know about this. Also, I'm sorry, but I'll be having Clarisse fill in as TA for your tutorial session."

"No!" Sam bolted upright. "I need this job, Professor Anderson. Please. I made a mistake, it won't happen again. I'll call a locksmith and stay here all night if I have to, I'll have them replace everything and I'll pay for it."

"You have the money for that, son?" Colin couldn't help but feel a little pity for the kid.

Hearing Ginny's readiness to kick Colin off the job sparked a memory of Colin's own distraction-caused mistake with the Service. The difference was that his mistake had cost someone their life. Sam's mistake hadn't done damage of nearly that caliber, so far as they knew, but he recognized the desperation in the young man's voice.

He'd heard it from himself the day he'd been called into the deputy director's office and dismissed from the job that had meant everything to him.

Sam sputtered something about student loans and working extra hours and teaching assistant duties to cover the expense, but Colin held up his hand to still the flood. "Professor Anderson and I will speak to the dean about this. Finish up your shift here for now and we'll talk more later."

Colin took Ginny's upper arm and led her away from the desk, back to her tiny office. He winced internally at the disbelief on her face and the redness around her eyes.

"Think you may have overstepped your bounds a little bit on that one, Mr. Tapping?"

Colin sighed. "The kid made a mistake. No need to fire him completely. Put him on probation for a while or take away one of his tutorial classes or something, but don't punish him for trying to help someone."

"His girlfriend?"

"You're telling me you never leave your office to get a cup of coffee? What if the keys had disappeared while he'd gone to the washroom or been holding the door open for a delivery? Circumstances make his actions look grimmer and more severe than they are. It was a dumb move for him to not keep the keys with him, but he had no reason to suspect they'd go missing. Besides, what would someone want with access to your department if they already believed you'd hand over your research documents?"

Ginny pursed her lips and looked around her trashed office. "Our computers are all pretty old, thanks to constant budget cuts. There's not much in the way of artifacts or ancient stuff in here. Not anything of value at all. The archaeology professor down the hall has a separate lab that's accessed with the master key, but she has most everything locked up in there in private cabinets. Plus, it's all pottery fragments and figurine pieces anyway, nothing valuable on the black market."

Colin crossed the room and surveyed the damage. "Can you tell if they took anything?"

Several beats of silence passed as Ginny

gazed at the mess of papers and books strewn about her office. In the far corner, a potted plant had been overturned, its roots now exposed to the air and its leaves crumpled under the weight of its formerly life-giving soil. "Nothing jumps out at me. I'd like to think this is unrelated to what happened outside, but I suppose that's ridiculous to even consider."

"Agreed. Unless you know of a jealous colleague who's prone to breaking and entering?"

"Jealous colleague?" Ginny's voice grew quiet. "There's one other professor here who may also be eligible for the tenure-track position, but I haven't even met the woman. I can't see her considering me a rival without having ever said hello."

That's what Colin was afraid of. Ginny seemed like the kind of person who saw the best in others, even when they gave her a reason not to. "I think we'll want to make meeting her a priority."

"The computer!" Ginny knelt and crawled under her desk, leaving Colin to decipher the non sequitur. She dragged the computer tower out from where it lay on its side under the desk, a wince of pain on her face.

Colin joined her on the floor and gently nudged her hands aside. "You just got knocked to the ground by a homemade bomb. Take it easy." Their eyes locked and she gave a slight gasp before standing. Colin swallowed down the sudden surprise of how cold her fingers were. And the electric spark that seemed to alight upon contact.

That wouldn't do. Would not do at all.

He trained his focus on the computer tower, flipping it around to look inside the back. "Looks like your hunch was right. The hard drive is gone." He risked a glance at her, but she'd bent over to retrieve something on the floor.

"It doesn't matter," she said.

"Doesn't matter?" He stood, noticing she'd cupped her palms together. "What about your research?"

Her voice dropped volume further, hitching on the words. "I only use cloud storage these days...more secure..."

Colin's heart constricted at her tone. He automatically reached out to offer a light touch of comfort to her wrist, but she pulled away and opened her palms. Her little fish lay cupped in her palms, lying still. "Oh, Ginny, you should have said something."

She shook her head and swallowed hard, blinking back tears. "Figuring out who did this is more important. I only hope... I hope Tigris didn't suffer when whoever did this threw his bowl on the floor..."

The impulse to do something, anything, to stop her sadness spurred a memory buried deep in his childhood psyche. "Wait here. Don't move."

Colin grabbed the fishbowl from the floor and scooped up some of the stones and aquarium plants, then ran a few steps down the hall to the staff room. He opened cupboards at random until he found what he was looking for—room-temperature bottled water. He dumped three bottles of water into the fishbowl and sped back to a bewildered Ginny. "Put him in here."

"But he's stiff. He's been out of water too long."

"Trust me. Put him in the water."

She frowned, but gently lowered the little fish into the bowl. Several tense moments passed as they both watched the bowl in silence, Colin praying that his childhood memories of his parents' fish tanks hadn't betrayed him.

Tigris wiggled, his little gills moving slowly as his natural breathing returned. Colin released the breath he'd been holding and looked up to see Ginny staring at her fish in disbelief.

"How is that possible? I thought fish couldn't survive out of water for more than a few minutes."

Colin set the bowl down on her desk where she could keep a close eye on it as she cleaned the place up. "Betta fish have something called a labyrinth organ that allows them to breathe air for a short period of time, even up to several hours. I suspect he wasn't out of water for anywhere near that length of time, so I imagine he'll be fine. You'll want to change the water in his bowl and treat it as usual as soon as possible, but he's going to be okay."

"That's amazing. When I saw his bowl on the floor, I thought the worst. Thank you." Without warning, she reached out and hugged him, but immediately pulled back and stared at the floor as though embarrassed by this sudden display of emotion. Standing this close, he could see a hint of the redness on her hidden cheek through the loose strands of shiny blond hair that attempted to cover it up. His curiosity nearly got the better of him, but he shoved aside the question. There were far more important issues to focus on, and Ginny needed to get checked over by a nurse. Plus, he'd promised to take the original letter and envelope down to the police station.

They needed to figure out what was really

going on and do it fast, because one thing had become abundantly clear this afternoon—whoever wanted Ginny's research was getting desperate.

Ginny checked her rearview mirror as she pulled into her apartment building's parking garage, seeing Colin's car on the street a few lengths behind hers. Nurse, police, hospital visit to Donna. All with Colin in tow, the man constantly checking corners and exits and all the while insisting Ginny remain within arm's length. He'd then insisted on accompanying her home and checking the apartment over for security flaws. She had faith that the police would figure it out and connect the dots between the attacks and demands on her research—and she appreciated Colin's dedication to her safety—but this was a bit much, wasn't it?

He parked in one of the few visitors' spots outside the garage and then joined her in taking the stairs up to the eighth floor.

"Remind me again why we can't take the elevator?" Ginny huffed, feeling a twinge in her knees from the impact of hitting the ground earlier. Colin took the stairs ahead of her, making it look easy. The man was in peak physical condition, which she kept trying not to notice. He didn't make *that* easy at all.

"There's little security in taking an elevator from the ground floor. Too easy for an ambush. If you're hurting, though, I'd feel safe taking it up the final few floors. Everything seems clear so far."

She appreciated his concern and almost agreed, but the sudden thought of the elevator doors yawning open reminded her of the open van doors earlier that morning. Had it really happened less than twelve hours ago? This day seemed never ending. Ginny gritted her teeth and pushed through the pain. "I can make it."

When they reached her apartment, Colin motioned for her to hand him the keys. "Here's how we do this. There's no sign of forced entry, but I'm not willing to make assumptions. I enter and begin a sweep, you come inside behind me and stand to the left of the doorway. You'll be out of sight from anyone in the hallway and allow for a fast exit if there's trouble. Make sense?"

Ginny nodded and leaned against the wall to ease the pressure in her aching legs. One small mercy was that she hadn't had to endure that climb while also trying to lug the bag of heavy tablets. As per the agreement with the Ashmore Museum and the Kingdom of Amar, they were locked tight inside a heavy-duty cabinet in the school's archaeology lab.

With her assent, Colin drew his gun, unlocked the door and swung it open. Ginny followed close behind as he entered, stepping aside as instructed once past the doorway. She leaned against the wall. Could Colin hear her heart pounding in her chest? She wanted to believe Colin was overreacting by searching her apartment, but his intensity had rubbed off and now she couldn't shake the fear.

Might it have something to do with almost getting abducted and blown up? She suddenly felt very, very tired, as if her energy had been siphoned away and left her dry. She blinked away the descending fog of sleepiness as Colin returned to the common room.

"No one here, nothing looks amiss," he said. He tucked his gun back into the waistband of his pants, then brushed aside a set of curtains at a nearby window. "Unless you see anything I didn't. You know the contents of your place better than anyone."

"Lord willing, this can be a safe haven for me tonight."

"I'm sure God has better things to do than patrol your apartment."

She heard the hurt in his voice. "You'd be surprised." As much as she'd like to ask him more questions about that reaction, she wasn't sure she could stay upright even one moment longer. She needed a cup of tea and chance to put her feet up. No more running around for a little while. "Thanks for looking around. I'll do a quick walk-through, but I don't see anything immediately concerning. Does that mean you get to go home tonight?"

He shook his head and checked out the other window. "Doubtful."

"But...but you can't stay here," she said, stumbling over the words. That would be taking "within arm's length" way too far.

"Of course not." He left the window and crossed the room toward her, the first hint of a smile she'd seen on his face nearly all day. It suited him, those hard edges softened and the crease in his forehead all but gone. "I want to think you'll be unbothered tonight, but I'm not about to make another errant assumption after today. I thought I could get a step ahead of this guy."

"Or woman."

"Yes, or woman. But I didn't. I made a mistake and you could have been seriously injured. I underestimated the intelligence of our opponent and the kind of reach this person has with their resources." He paused, tension returning to his jaw. "I should know better."

"But how could you have? Your plan was solid. Even the police agreed to it. You couldn't have anticipated what happened."

"Except that's what I'm trained to do. I promise you, I won't make that mistake again."

Judging by his expression, she believed him, but after today he probably needed a moment of rest as badly as she did. "Do you want a cup of tea before you go?" She hoped he'd take the hint one way or the other. "Since you can't stay here."

Colin sighed, hard edges softening again. "Sure. It'll give me time to consider the best way to keep an eye on you tonight."

Ginny set her electric kettle to boil, then pulled two tea bags from a tin on the counter. She set out two mugs, milk and sugar. After a minute, the kettle still hadn't boiled yet. Well, she had a rack full of dishes to put away, so she might as well use the time to be productive.

A chill slithered down her spine as she lifted a plate out of the dish rack. Shoved sideways in the space between her plates was another nondescript envelope. Here. In her *home*.

"Colin?" She tried to keep the waver out of her voice, without success. "I found something." Using a dishcloth, Ginny pulled the envelope out of the dish rack. It was the exact same size and color as the envelope that had arrived at the department office earlier that afternoon. A familiar label on the front listed her name only. No stamp, no return address, no other identifiers.

Colin entered the kitchen just in time to catch her as her legs buckled. The exhaustion of the day combined with this violation in her own home was too much.

"Easy there. Let's get you to a chair before you hurt yourself." Strong arms slipped around her waist and shoulders. She couldn't even muster the energy to protest as Colin guided her to the couch and eased her down. "Want me to open it?"

She choked back a wave of emotion in response, slid the edge of the dishcloth on her finger and under the envelope's sealed flap to tear it open. Then, holding down the envelope with the hem of her shirt so as to not touch the paper, she used the cloth to slide out a piece of paper the same size and texture as the letter she'd received earlier today. As before, the words looked to have been punched onto the paper by typewriter keys striking the page.

It appears you are a well-connected woman, Professor Anderson. While I do not appreciate your attempts to thwart the terms of our agreement, I do hope that my small gift this afternoon clarified the extent of my reach. Surely you understand there are consequences for every action. Should you attempt to set another trap for me and my associates, I shall turn it again in my favor.

However, I am a generous individual and shall consider today's events an effort at negotiation. I have significant resources at my disposal and shall present a counteroffer.

Five hundred thousand dollars on the terms mentioned in my previous correspondence. You will collect the aforementioned documents and place them inside this envelope. Leave the envelope on the top of the soda machine located inside the west-facing doors of the Student Services building at four o'clock tomorrow afternoon. I assure you, no incendiary device will accost your personage should you follow these instructions. On this occasion, I advise you to forgo the protective muscle.

As previously mentioned, tardiness is inadvisable. Negotiations are now complete. Idleness begets consequences, Professor. You would do the same for a petulant student. Consider me the teacher in this particular instance.

Please refer to the enclosed for evidence of the particulars.

"Efforts at negotiation?"

Colin grimaced. "Sometimes I hate being right. This is a back-and-forth game for our opponent. They took the advantage today and they know it. Is there something else inside? What's the enclosed evidence they talked about?"

There was something else in the envelope, but Ginny couldn't bring herself to reach inside again. She already felt dizzy, and the waves of exhaustion had returned. "Can you do it?"

Colin took the dishcloth and the envelope, then turned it upside down. Two photographs tumbled from inside. The first, a photo of Colin and Ginny visiting Donna in the hospital a little over four hours ago. The second, a photo of Ginny's apartment building. Her eighth-story apartment had been circled with red marker. Their opponent knew exactly where she lived and somehow had gotten inside her home to leave this here, sending a clear message: nowhere was safe.

SEVEN

"Pack whatever things you'll need overnight," Colin said. He slid the photos and the letter back into the envelope. "Do you have anyone you could call who might allow you to stay with them tonight?"

Ginny blinked at him in bewilderment, complexion pale.

"Ginny, we need to get you out of here tonight. It's not safe. This individual knows exactly where your apartment is and found a way to access it. We already know they managed to steal keys from your department's reception desk, so it's not inconceivable that they'd manage the same thing here somehow. Is there a security system here? I can have the police request the footage from the manager—"

He heard himself rambling and yet couldn't seem to stop. Ginny's blank expression unnerved him. "Ginny?"

She blinked again. Her chest barely rose and

fell with each breath. Alarm constricted his insides. She could be going into shock.

"Stay with me, Virginia." He took her limp hand, pressing her cold fingers between his own. She didn't flinch or shy away, but did shift her gaze to him. Good. A response, at least. "I don't want to stick around here any longer than necessary," he told her. "Is there someplace you can stay overnight?"

"No," she whispered. "My family lives too far away. Maybe if there's a dorm room available?"

"Go pack. I'll figure it out." Hotel it was. They'd have to drop by the police station first, and maybe someone there could recommend a safe place to put her up until this was over. A threat in her own home raised the stakes in a significant way. They knew how to get to Ginny and weren't afraid to brag about it with photographic evidence.

Intimidation and fear were strong, effective weapons. Good thing neither tactic worked on a fully trained agent of the Secret Service, active or not. No one deserved this kind of treatment while simply trying to do a job, regardless of whether the opposition disagreed with a policy, an action or perceived perspective. In fact, one of the reasons Colin had joined the Service in the first place had stemmed from a strong desire to protect those who had dedicated themselves to bettering the lives of others. Presidents, diplomats and now a young female college professor from this small Pennsylvania college.

Ginny slipped off the couch in silence and returned a few moments later with a small duffel bag in hand. Her right shoulder sagged, and Colin felt like a bit of an idiot for not realizing that her shoulder had to also hurt from lugging the heavy tablets around all day. If only she'd been able to negotiate a better transportation arrangement—but from what she'd told him, even arranging to have them at all had been difficult enough for Curator Wehbe.

"Where are we going?" She looked over her shoulder at the apartment windows, frowning. "Are you sure it's safe to leave?"

Truthfully, he wasn't convinced the person behind the letters and the attacks—or their lackeys—wouldn't be waiting nearby to see what she'd do after receiving this new message, but staying here was not an option. "I won't let anything happen to you. I promise."

She grimaced as he stepped forward to take the duffel bag from her grasp. He slung the strap over his head as she folded her arms across her stomach. "Promise all you want,

Mr. Tapping, but if you don't mind, I'm going to rely on God's protection first."

Colin scoffed. "Does God have a gun? Can He shoot the bad guys?"

The barest hint of a smile appeared on her lips, a brief flash of the Ginny he'd met earlier today. Had he really met her only last night... only twenty-four hours ago?

"I never said that God didn't send *you* to be that protection," she said.

If Ginny was relying on him to be her God-sent protection, well, where had He been two years ago when Lynn Gustav had done the same?

Ginny followed Colin into the hallway, grateful that he'd taken the burden of the duffel bag for her. Her nerves were on edge, causing a strange floating sensation thanks to the combination of exhaustion and adrenaline. She'd also barely eaten anything all day due to the nonstop rush from one place to another, and her empty stomach made her feel nauseated.

"Stay behind me," Colin instructed. He walked forward with his gun drawn and pointed down at the floor. "Once we reach the stairwell, we move quickly and quietly. Go fast, but also listen for any noises out of place."

She swallowed a wave of anxiety and followed in silence. As they entered the stairwell, he glanced back and nodded at her, a gesture that she returned. She was ready to get out of here and find someplace to rest. If anyone could get her out safely, he could. Had God brought Colin to her life to do just that? Navigating all of this on her own today would have been impossible. She'd probably be in the hospital right next to Donna if he hadn't been around. She remained amazed at Colin's determination and willingness to protect her today without a single complaint or ounce of hesitation.

Certainly instinct and training were the only reasons. After all, he'd looked far too surprised when he'd accidentally touched her ruined cheek last night, and she'd seen that look before. She'd dated several nice guys over the years who'd seemed like gentlemen and who'd told her she was beautiful. She hadn't realized they were so shallow and rude until she'd fallen for them and decided she could trust them. Each time, when she'd finally pulled back the hair that covered her injury, those guys had flinched and given her a tight smile. *Everything's fine*, they'd said. *You're still lovely. I can get used to it.* As though her injury wasn't a part of her. As though it was some kind of hurdle to get over rather than accept.

She wasn't willing to go through that again. It hurt too much, and in any case, she and Colin were colleagues. She couldn't allow herself to think of him as anything beyond the protector role he'd slipped into on her behalf.

They traversed the first five flights of stairs without incident, but when Colin froze on the third-floor landing, Ginny bumped into his shoulder. "Sorry," she whispered.

He shook his head and tapped his ear. Ginny strained to hear anything unusual, but couldn't make out any sound over the thud of her own heart.

And then she *did* hear it. A click, like the latch of a door catching. Followed by more silence. Colin pointed above them, then motioned for her to get in front of him. He leaned in so close she felt the heat of his breath as he whispered one word.

"Run."

Her blood turned cold as she gripped the handrails and half ran, half slid down the next flight of steps, a second wind of adrenaline pumping through her veins. She felt Colin's presence right behind her and heard a tap of feet on stairs high above them.

Ginny slammed the door open to the parking garage's ground floor, then veered right to run out of the garage and toward Colin's car as planned, but Colin's hand clamped around her forearm and pulled her toward her hatchback.

"Yours is closer," he explained. "Dig out those keys and let's go. I'll drive."

"I can drive," she protested, pawing through her small purse for her key ring.

Colin plucked the keys from her hand as she held them aloft. "I want you to get in the back and lie down."

He climbed into the driver's seat and she followed his instructions. "Why am I doing this?"

"Hang on. You secure back there?" Colin threw the car into Reverse as she clicked her seat belt shut. "Whoever's after you knows what your car looks like, remember? Sitting up here or driving will make you a target."

She peeked over the edge of the passenger window as Colin accelerated out of the parking garage and down the driveway. No one had come through the stairwell door yet, but what if they did? What if they were armed?

What if it had only been another building resident deciding to take the stairs as a health-conscious option and they'd been overreacting about the whole thing?

As Colin pulled out onto the road, Ginny saw a brief flash of light from the bushes half a block away. "Did you see that?"

"We're being watched," Colin said. He yanked

on the steering wheel and pulled a U-turn, heading away from the flash of light.

"What do you think that was?" Ginny tried to swallow the lump in her throat.

"A reflection. Binoculars or some other kind of scope."

Ginny heard the hesitation in his voice as he kept glancing in the rearview mirror. She got the impression that if she hadn't been in the car with him, he'd have driven toward the flash of light rather than away from it. Worry gnawed at her stomach as they drove, the adrenaline of the past few minutes beginning to wear off.

"Colin, I don't understand what's going on. Why do these people want my work? Why do they think I'd give it up for any amount of money?"

"There are some people in this world who believe…no, scratch that." He banged his hand against the steering wheel before continuing. "Everyone has a price, Ginny. The right amount hasn't been offered yet, but these people are trying to give it to you. No, hold on. Just listen. If someone offered you five million dollars, you might think differently, right? But the fact is that this money they're offering, and any subsequent offer, has come with a threat attached."

"I don't follow."

"Honestly, if there'd been no threat? No attempted kidnapping, no grenade? Truthfully, I might tell you to consider the offer. That's a lot of money on a part-timer's salary. Under different circumstances, you might be able to negotiate a great deal for your and their rights to your future work, but with all this baggage attached, there's more at stake than purely losing your research. We're going to take this letter and photo to the police together and figure out where to go from there."

Ginny pushed herself up to a more comfortable seated position, resting her head in the sling of the seat belt cross-strap. "It's the *why* that I don't get. Why me? Why *my* work? There's no real value here beyond knowledge, and there's no opposition to the work that I know of. I mean, the Amaran government sent a representative to help oversee my work, and if I find the right location for this summer palace, we're talking a massive tourism boost. Once it's dug up, of course, but the long-term benefits will be extensive for such a small country."

"Then we need to look elsewhere. Find out who could benefit from your research being halted before this goes any further."

Ginny laughed without humor. "Then we'd better get on it. The second drop is tomorrow afternoon, right? We can't try the same thing again and they know it. What if they get ahead of us tomorrow, too?"

Colin's jaw tightened and Ginny finally saw the etched lines of weariness around his eyes. The day had taken a toll on him, too. She hoped they'd both be able to get some rest tonight, because tomorrow wasn't shaping up to be much better.

He sighed and glanced at her in the mirror, her throat closing with anxiety at his answer. "I honestly have no idea, Ginny. And that's what I'm afraid to find out."

EIGHT

Colin's first stop had to be the police station, where Ginny could hand over the letter and photos and give a statement. The woman looked dead on her feet. Getting her to a place where she could rest was a priority, but first he needed to talk to someone with authority on the local police force. He'd established a good relationship with the local cops so far, but if the goodwill didn't extend upward, the dicier the situation became, the more difficult it'd be to keep Ginny safe.

The receptionist led him and Ginny to a side room with mismatched chairs and a cozy-looking couch. Ginny sank into it as Colin poured them both cups of coffee from a pot set up outside the door. She gratefully accepted the mug and dumped three packets of sugar into it without hesitation.

Several minutes and a half-empty coffee

mug later, the police chief entered the room, easily identified as such by his uniform.

"Chief Walter Black," the man said. "You're Colin Tapping, I presume?"

Colin nodded and tried to match the chief's tone. "Correct. Former Secret Service, Counter Assault Team and Presidential Protective Detail. Marine before that." He didn't intend to brag by listing credentials, but the chief needed to know he could have confidence in Colin. "With me is Professor Virginia Anderson, the woman who's kind of had a rough day."

"Bit of an understatement, I'd say. My boys have told me all about you, Tapping. There's been some buzz around the office about your position up at the college. What brings you to our small town?"

That was a discussion he'd prefer not to have right now, not with more important things at stake. And truth be told, his past could be either a boon or a curse, depending on how the chief viewed government law enforcement—and Colin had met both types in local police departments.

"Sometimes the stress of the job gets the better of a man," Colin said. How the chief reacted would let him know whether the man knew the circumstances of Colin's departure or not. "Mistakes are made, and it's time to start over."

Chief Black thumped his fist on the back of a chair. "Don't I know it, Tapping. Don't I know it. Look, it's good to see a government man making something of himself after, well, you know."

Ah, so he did know after all. "Can't sit around, don't believe in giving in to vices. Only thing left is to move on and keep living."

Chief Black waved at Colin to take a seat. The chief closed the door as Colin sat down, then joined them, hands folded across his knees. "Since this isn't a social call, I'll get to the point. Officer Carlton has kept me updated on what's been happening up at the school. Military grenade, attempted kidnapping, possible bribery, homemade explosives and several break-and-enters. Sounds like a mess, Tapping."

"A second letter arrived tonight at Miss Anderson's apartment, a direct response to what transpired this afternoon. Did you take a look at the one I passed your officers earlier today?"

"I did. And you're certain these letters are connected to the library incident and the attempted kidnapping?"

"I think that's the best explanation we've got, Chief. The first letter referenced the kidnapping but neither has talked about the library, which makes me think the library incident was pre-meditated. I don't think it was a success for whoever pulled it off, but it sounds like the kidnapping in contrast was the result of some overly enthusiastic lackeys. I know the grenade was military issue—which is the really odd factor when you consider the incendiary device tossed at us earlier was a fast home build, easily put together in minutes with the right materials. We seem to have a highly intelligent opportunist on our hands. I talked with Officer Carlton earlier, and he agrees. It's like someone hired out a retrieval or hit contract to unvetted criminals and is calling shots on the fly."

The chief chuckled. "It's not like someone hiring out for this kind of work asks for a résumé."

"You've got that right. Did your boys also mention the professor's hard drive was stolen? She doesn't have anything sensitive on it, but it's maybe notable. The perp went for outdated storage tech and is sending paper letters. I don't think our guy or lady likes or understands technology all that much."

"Wouldn't be the first time. Miss Anderson, do you know of anyone who might fit this description? Doesn't have a full grasp on tech, likes to outsource work, tied to old ways of doing things? Too smart for their own good?"

Ginny glanced over the top of her mug, a bitter laugh on her lips. "I work in a history department of a college, sir. That description matches basically every single person I interact with daily."

Colin cleared his throat to pull back the chief's attention. "And the letter writer knows where Miss Anderson lives. Until this second letter we had no direct threats, but the manner in which the letter was delivered—dropped right in her apartment, with photos inside that show she was being observed today—is disturbing."

"Agreed. I'll send forensics over to look for prints, but I know we didn't find anything on the first letter. We'll check the second, too. She needs a place to stay tonight?"

"Hoping you can recommend a place, Chief."

"Talk to Wanda at the front desk. She'll give you the address of a place visiting officers stay. It's just down the road. Need a detail to watch her?"

Colin raised an eyebrow, unable to pull back the immediate sarcasm in his expression. He kept his tone neutral, hoping not to offend while still getting his point across. "I've no doubt your officers are all fine policemen, but when it comes to experience with protection?"

The chief waved his hand and sat back in the chair. "Yes, yes. I know. Elite training for one of the highest-regarded protection organizations in the world. I have a feeling that being a civilian these days hasn't changed much of anything for you, huh?"

The chief got it. He really got it, and that was as much of a relief as anything right now. "No, sir."

Chief Black looked over his shoulder, then back at Colin, gaze intense. "I know you know the law, Tapping. And you're no longer an active agent."

"Correct."

"But I also know you're trained to do what's needed. And my boys tend to be a little loose with information around you. As long as I don't see you walking in here in cuffs...we understand each other?"

"Loud and clear, Chief."

They both stood and shook hands again. With the chief out of the room, Colin sank into the couch next to Ginny for a brief moment of respite.

She looked bemused. "I'm not sure I followed that."

Colin rubbed his face with his hands, relieved that the chief hadn't tried to wrest control from him. Working together, he and the local police force would be that much more effective. So long as the Secret Service kept their end of the bargain and had his back.

"We're going to catch the bad guy," he said, with more confidence than he actually felt. Without enough evidence to figure out what was going on, the best strategy was to wait and see what would happen next—and hope the letter writer got impatient and tipped his hand.

The only problem with that approach was that they had no idea how it could play out. What if their opponent tipped his hand too far and harmed Ginny again in the process?

"Thanks for hanging around last night," Ginny said, climbing into her car the following morning. Colin sat at the wheel. Since they hadn't ventured back to her compromised apartment to retrieve Colin's vehicle, he'd apparently spent the night in her car outside the motel door, watching over her. "Did you get any rest at all?"

"Chief Black sent a uniform to spell me for a few hours. Our cars traded places for a bit."

Though she was still physically tired, an overnight rest had removed the fog of yesterday's events and renewed her strength to face the day. "That's not nearly enough. You'll keel over by morning."

He laughed, a happy sound on an uncertain morning. "Sleep deprivation was a regular part of being an agent. I've done plenty of twelve-hour overnight shifts where I've gone home to get rest after, only to be called back in because the president or whoever changed their plans and they needed more personnel to cover it."

Ginny couldn't imagine being under that kind of pressure and being sleep deprived. "That's dedication. I find it hard enough to function on less than seven hours of solid rest. And even that needs caffeine afterward."

He started up the car. "Then let's find you some before we get this day under way." Her heart skipped a beat as he glanced over and smiled at her.

Stop it. It's nothing personal, Ginny. His actions were simply part of what he knew how to do: protect. *He's doing this to try to get his job back. It's not about you.*

Drive-through breakfast sandwiches and coffees in hand, Colin took them the rest of the way to Gwyn Ponth. He parked on a small side road, out of the way from the main parking area. "I know you have important things to do today, and I'm not going to stop you, but

I'm going to do whatever I can to reduce the potential risk of being on campus."

That wasn't what she expected at all. "Really? Why not just lock me in the motel until this is figured out?"

"Because you have me." He paused as though deciding what to say next. "Watching your back, I mean. Look, let me put it like this. When the president of the United States wants to go for a run around downtown DC during morning rush hour, what do you think the Secret Service does?"

Ginny had no idea, but it sounded like a ridiculous proposition. "That seems terribly unsafe. Surely you tell him he has to use an indoor track or a more secure area?"

Colin shook his head. "Nope. We accommodate. We have as many agents as needed along the route, plus someone to run with him. I know some law enforcement teams and agencies are all about hiding people away, but that's no way to live. How would you like being cooped up all day? You'd never get your important work done and you'd feel like a prisoner. That's why people like me have the training we do. Nothing less than perfection is expected from us, because that's the only way we can guarantee your safety and allow you to conduct your necessary business."

"But you're not Secret Service anymore."

His features grew dark and the lighthearted moment they'd shared earlier evaporated. "For one moment, I forgot to be perfect."

"I didn't mean—"

"Forget it. Let's go."

It had come out all wrong. That's not what she'd meant at all—was it? Or had she intentionally antagonized him because he was getting too comfortable to be around?

They walked in silence to the Daviau Center, regret churning in her stomach, yet she was unable to think of what to say to make things right. Instead, she turned her thoughts to the day's appointment with Dr. Hilden. The man had seemed very enthusiastic about the work yesterday and even requested that she make a copy of her notes for him to personally send to the University of Amar back home. If she made the summer palace discovery, would they invite her to come speak in Amar? Maybe she'd get to meet the archaeological team that would head out to the dig site, or maybe she'd even get to help head it up herself. In a consultation role, of course. She was no archaeologist. That field of study was a whole different and complex ball game.

Mrs. McCall, the department receptionist, was back at her desk this morning. She waved cheerily as Ginny and Colin approached. "Morning, sweetie. I hear things got a little exciting yesterday."

Ginny groaned and rested her bags on the floor. "You heard? I guess you had to, what with the lock getting changed last night and all."

"Wouldn't you believe it. Oh, a few students stopped by to hand in papers this morning. I slipped them into the box next to your door. Beverly Dorn also stopped by a little while ago, but I told her you were out."

Ginny frowned. "Who's Beverly Dorn?"

"That's me," came a silky-smooth voice behind her. Ginny whirled around to see an immaculately dressed, elegant, age forty-something woman crossing the department common area toward her. The woman's black heels were muffled against the carpeted floor, but Ginny had a feeling they'd be the kind of shoes that clicked loudly wherever this woman walked. Her chin-length black hair was straight, symmetrical and reminded Ginny of wigs she'd seen on department store mannequins.

Ginny offered what she hoped was a friendly smile, but the woman didn't return the expression. When Ginny stretched out her hand to greet Beverly, the woman's eyes spared Ginny's palm the briefest of glances before ignoring it entirely. Her gaze slipped past Colin as though he didn't exist.

"Dr. Beverly Dorn," the woman said. "But Professor Dorn will also do."

"Whatever you say, Bev," mumbled Mrs. McCall, loud enough for only Ginny to hear.

Ginny suppressed a laugh and folded her arms across her chest, since *Dr.* Dorn clearly had no intention of engaging in common social gestures. "By process of elimination, I assume you're the new Italian prof?"

"Certainly," the woman said with a sniff. Her eyes traveled up and down Ginny's figure, as though sizing her up. Ginny shifted uncomfortably. She hadn't bothered to shower this morning at the motel and she looked like a grubby mess. Of course she'd have to meet the elegant Italian professor today of all days. "So. You and I are in competition?"

"For tenure track, yes," Ginny said, glancing back at Mrs. McCall with eyebrows raised. "But I wouldn't call it competition. We're colleagues, and it's ultimately up to the college to decide who they believe has more potential to become a valuable permanent member of the staff."

Beverly's face remained flat and impassive. "Indeed it is."

Who did this woman think she was? No,

Ginny scolded herself, that wasn't fair. Maybe the woman had issues with social cues, or maybe she was a shy person who overcompensated with coldness. It didn't mean that she was being rude on purpose, even if it seemed that way.

"Ginny's doing some exciting research on an ongoing project," Mrs. McCall piped in. "She's studying some ancient tablets to support some of her published theories. She might discover the location of an ancient palace, isn't that exciting?"

Ginny felt heat rush to her cheeks. She wasn't sure whether to thank Mrs. McCall or beg her to stop. Her work wasn't *that* exciting…all right, that wasn't true. She loved it, despite her mother's feelings on her chosen career path.

Beverly's eyebrows raised and she tut-tutted. "Oh, dear. I'm so sorry."

"What?" Ginny couldn't stop herself from blurting it out. "What's that supposed to mean?"

"You haven't heard? Oh, my. One should really keep up on current events, particularly as they pertain to one's life's work, don't you think?"

Ginny glanced back at Mrs. McCall and Colin, suddenly feeling frantic, but the receptionist only shrugged. She looked almost as confused as Ginny felt. Had something happened to the museum? Or to Dr. Hilden?

When Ginny didn't respond, Beverly laced her fingers together in front of her stomach and looked down her nose at the other woman. "I've heard of your work, of course, Miss Anderson. One must keep abreast of their competition's progress in some way, but it seems that someone else has done that for me. Surely you've heard that the land you've posited as a possible location for the ancient summer palace has been sold."

Ginny's stomach dropped into her toes as she and Colin blurted the same thing at the same time. "What?"

"You really haven't heard this? Dear me. The details of the sale have yet to be released, but it happened a few days ago. Don't you read world news? Really, my dear. You should keep track of these things."

Sold? The possible location of an ancient historical site had been *sold*? To *whom*? "That's impossible," she said, the words slipping out as tiny squeaks.

A dark, thin smile spread slowly across Beverly's face. "Not at the right price."

NINE

As he had yesterday, Colin stood in Ginny's office doorway, keeping an eye out for anything amiss—but unlike yesterday, he was having a harder time concentrating. As if meeting the snooty Beverly Dorn hadn't left enough of a bad taste in his mouth, the poor woman sitting behind him looked as though the world had come crashing down upon her shoulders. He had a strange longing to say or do something that would erase the distress from her lovely features, but verbal reassurance had never been one of his strengths.

After forty minutes of enduring silence, he couldn't take it any longer. "Are you going to be okay? Do you need to take the rest of the day off?"

When Ginny didn't respond, he followed her eyes to the screen. She was reading an article from the *Amaran Daily News Online*, written in English, about the sale of a piece of land to an unnamed corporation. The story described the terms of the sale but failed to note the amount or the purchaser. According to the article, the nature of the sale was under a confidentiality agreement until the final papers were signed.

"The land should belong to the Amaran people," Ginny finally said. "I've already published preliminary reports about this area and how there might be extremely important historical sites buried here. And the government of Amar knows it, because they sent Dr. Hilden here to consult with me on the tablets. How could this happen?"

"This could be a good thing," he offered. "It doesn't say who bought the land, so there's no need to think the worst. It could have been the University of Amar or an archaeological company."

Ginny turned a frustrated eye on him. "You don't know how these things work, do you? Not disclosing the nature of the sale until its completion means that someone doesn't want anyone to know so that there won't be attempts to block the sale."

"Don't they have to disclose it? It's public land, right?"

"Amar isn't the United States, Colin. Things work differently in other countries, especially countries in the developing world. The rules aren't the same."

Colin knew that, but he'd hoped that his words would ease her fears a little bit. "That still doesn't mean that you need to think the worst."

Ginny went silent for a few moments, then swung her chair around so she faced him. "Amar is an oil-rich nation. It's also the kind of country where foreign companies like to invest and build expensive buildings or tourism resorts. A small country like that needs all the financial help it can get, because the wealth from oil doesn't always trickle down into the rest of the population. And if it's the choice of a massive cash influx versus waiting for a possible historical and archaeological discovery that might not even happen—and, if it does, for which the financial return won't happen for many years—it's not hard to see where the government's choice would fall."

Sadly, Colin understood all too well how these kinds of politics worked, and he agreed with her. If the details weren't revealed, it likely meant the buyer feared blowback from the sale. "You think the buyer knows about your work?"

"Me? A little ancient languages and history professor in Pennsylvania? I doubt it. They probably just want to avoid protestors picketing the area or the desert tribes raising a stink. Those tribes still live out there in the desert areas, and if they decide to hold a blockade, the international community is sure to hear about it. No doubt the company wants to quietly pay off the desert tribes once they have the rights to the land."

"The desert people don't own the land?"

Ginny shrugged. "Like I said, it's complicated. The Kingdom of Amar has a long history that stretches back thousands of years, so who owns what land generally falls under the discretion of the government and if needed, the ruling family."

"Messy. Makes me grateful for our system here in America."

Ginny raised an eyebrow at him. "It's different, I'll grant, but that doesn't make it worse or better. No one's being oppressed in Amar, no human rights have been violated—yet. God created us all in his own image, and so long as people are healthy, safe and maintain their basic rights, quibbling over the details is a waste of energy."

She made a good point, Colin had to admit, and he'd worked in the public sector long enough to see both the good and bad sides of a democratic government. Didn't mean he'd trade it for anything else, though. "Guess I'll have to settle for thanking God that I was born on this continent and leave it at that."

She wrinkled her nose in an adorable display of annoyance. "Fine. At least we can both agree that God's in control in one way or another, right?"

"I guess." Colin's pulse quickened as she turned her attention back to the computer screen. What was that about? He couldn't entertain those kinds of feelings. Her life and the lives and well-being of many Amaran people depended on her ability to complete this translation project. Even one moment without focus—

"Colin?"

Wrenched out of his thoughts, he found Ginny staring at him with narrowed eyes. "Yep. Right. Sorry. What?"

She inhaled and exhaled through her nose, her narrowed eyes closing farther. "You're staring at me."

He was? "Oh. I'm sorry, I was lost in thought. That's not my intention."

"Yes, I have a scar on my face. I know it's distracting, but don't you think I have enough to deal with right now?"

A gentle hand on his shoulder interrupted the sudden, bizarre shift the moment had taken.

He turned to see the head librarian, bandage around her head and wide smile on her face.

"You're the professor from Criminology who came with Ginny last night, yes?" she said.

"Donna!" Ginny stood and hugged her friend. "How are you feeling? I thought you'd be in the hospital for a few more days."

"Good to see you," Colin added, still stunned from Ginny's outburst. He'd hit a nerve without intending to, but hadn't she done the same to him this morning when discussing his past?

"Brought thank-you cookies," Donna said, handing over a blue plastic container.

Ginny took the container and lifted the lid. The scent of chocolate chip cookies caused Colin's mouth to water. "You baked? Shouldn't you be taking it easy?"

Donna waved off Ginny's concern and fluffed a stray strand of curly hair that had worked its way free from her bandage. "I'm sure you've heard that Roger left a note for me after finding out what happened? Well, we're finally going to meet in person. I have a dinner date!"

"That's nice," Colin said, momentarily glad for Donna's tension-dispersing presence. "Where is he taking you? And when?"

"Oh, I don't know." Donna waved her hands

dramatically. "He has quite the schedule as custodian here, so he's going to call me when he has the evening free. And I'm flexible. Either way, I have some of my own tricks up my sleeve. I'm going to surprise him with a little flight before dinner. Do you think he'll like it?"

Colin had no idea what the woman was talking about.

"Donna's a hobby pilot," Ginny explained. "Her family has a puddle jumper they use to scare people with."

"Not scare! It's exciting, being up there and flying free in the sky." Her voice took on a wistful tone and Colin marveled at the librarian's zest for life. Then again, most people had things about them that didn't come up in regular conversation. Like pilot's licenses. And old scars. And a death on their conscience. "I'll take you up sometime, Mr. Tapping. No thrill like it."

Of the thrill, he had no doubt—but he'd had quite his fill of excitement these past few days. Right now it was all he could do to prevent any more of it. What they really needed was a plan for the drop time this afternoon. No matter how much Ginny protested, he wouldn't allow her to volunteer herself into harm's way again.

* * *

After Donna left, Ginny wolfed down six chocolate chip cookies and nursed a stomach-ache for the rest of the morning. She didn't say anything to Colin, though—the man seemed worried enough about her without having to source anti-nausea tablets for her roiling insides. He hovered into the afternoon as she worked on the tablet translations in preparation for her meeting with Dr. Hilden in a few hours. Between Colin's presence and ongoing phone calls with the police station or campus security, and having learned about the land sale that morning, it became very difficult to concentrate.

She shouldn't have snapped at him earlier. He didn't deserve it, and in all likelihood he hadn't been staring at her face at all but just gazing blankly, lost in thought. The accusation had just slipped out, the product of her discomfort in the moment. Not discomfort at his presence. Discomfort at the strange, comfortable, soothing nature of having him around. It felt too normal to have him here by her side. She needed to shut that down immediately, before her heart became involved.

She heard him finish yet another phone conversation and got ready to apologize for her brusque rebuke. Before she took a breath, her TA Sam came barreling into the department.

"Professor Anderson! Professor Anderson!"

"Slow down, son." Colin placed a hand on the student's chest before he could barge into her little office. "What's going on?"

"It's your car! It's being towed."

Ginny shot out of her seat. "What do you mean? Colin parked us this morning." She shot an accusatory glare at Colin. "You parked us off campus on a side street. Did you even read the signs?"

"Of course I did," Colin growled. "How do you know, Sam?"

Sam huffed and puffed, bending over at the waist to catch his breath. "Another student… coming back from lunch…told me…tow truck, so I ran."

"Colin, I can't lose my car." Ginny grabbed her purse and dug out her keys, then groaned. She had the tablets out on her desk and couldn't leave them here unattended unless they were locked up in the lab. "You go." She tossed the keys to Colin. "Please?"

"I'm not leaving you here by yourself with the drop coming up."

"I have a meeting with Hilden. I'll pack up and go right over, right now."

"I can take her," Sam chimed in.

"Sorry, not good enough." Colin waved at the leather satchel. "Grab them and come with me. I'll walk you to the library after. Hurry!"

Ginny's shoulder ached just thinking about running all the way back to the car with the heavy tablet bag slung over the bruise that had formed there since yesterday. A sob welled up from deep inside. She couldn't afford to pay to get her car out of impound if they took it, and the fines for illegal street parking around campus were astronomical as a deterrent. "Colin, I can't run with these. They'll have to be locked up."

"Then you'd better move faster than that."

He took her keys into the archaeology lab and got the cabinet opened and ready for the satchel of tablets. Feeling the seconds slip by like hours, Ginny locked the bag in its secured home and followed Colin out the door.

She rushed across campus with him, expecting at any moment to see a tow truck pass by in the distance, her car trailing behind it. How could Colin have missed a parking sign? That didn't seem like him at all.

"Ginny, stop." Colin's hand fell on her shoulder as they rounded the southeast edge of campus.

Her car hadn't been towed. There it sat, a block away and undisturbed. No tow truck in sight. "Should we check the signs? Maybe the tow truck driver got it wrong." Ginny inhaled deeply to catch her breath as footsteps pounded behind them. Sam had followed, concern crossing his features.

"I'm sorry," he said, skidding to a stop beside them. "I didn't know if I should find you or go try to stop them myself."

Colin grabbed the front of the student's shirt. "Who told you it was being towed?"

Sam squealed as his feet nearly left the ground. "Another student!"

"Who?"

"I don't know," he protested. Ginny's sour stomach turned to lead. "Not someone I know, I assumed one of her students from another class. What's your problem, man?"

"Maybe there was a mistake. I can't be the only one who drives a blue hatchback." But when Ginny saw the look on Colin's face, she had to admit she was reaching. But why would someone do that, if not a mistake or a joke? "We know someone wants me to stop my research," she murmured. "And if I'm hesitant to do as they've asked, one way to encourage me to do it or force my hand would be…?"

The tablets.

"Colin, the tablets. We locked up the tablets, but…"

Colin released Sam and took off with her, running toward the Daviau Center with all the gas left in her tank. She yanked on the door, only to find it locked. Why would the building's outer door be locked at this time of day? There should be students coming and going, and they'd left here only minutes ago.

"Is there a faster entrance to the Language and Culture Department?" Colin paced in front of the door as she flipped through her key ring.

"No. This is the fastest way in." She fumbled to find the right key, each moment of delay seeming to take hours. Finally, she unlocked it and Colin yanked open the door. "The entrance on the other side of the building leads into the administrative area for the college. It'd take several minutes to get here from there."

"Great." Colin ran down the short hall to her department and yanked on that door. Also locked. "Was anyone else in here when we left? Besides the receptionist?"

Panic flared in Ginny's chest as she found the key. "I don't know. We talked to Beverly Dorn earlier, and it's possible there were others, but nearly everyone in this department teaches on Thursday afternoons."

Pounding from inside the office sent Colin into action. He ran inside the department and down toward the sound of the knocking. Instead of following him, Ginny headed to the receptionist's desk. Where was Mrs. McCall?

A high-pitched whine caught Ginny's ear. The phone was off the hook. Mrs. McCall would never leave the phone off the hook. Her hopes sank. Something was terribly wrong.

Ginny rounded the receptionist's desk and her stomach lurched into her throat. Mrs. McCall lay facedown on the floor, her limbs splayed out at unnatural angles. Some of her hair was red and matted, and streaks of red had dripped down her neck onto the floor. *Oh, no. Lord, please, no.*

She knelt and pressed two fingers to Mrs. McCall's neck, but her own pulse was racing too hard to tell if the prone woman's heart still beat.

And then Colin was next to her, one hand on her shoulder and the other hand on Mrs. McCall's throat. "Faint. Very faint, but if this just happened, we might be able to get an ambulance here in time."

"Call 911," Ginny shouted at Sam, who'd run into the department behind her. "Then call campus security, any emergency responders on campus and Foot Patrol. Have them announce that no one is to walk unescorted on campus right now. We may need a lockdown."

Sam looked stunned.

"Go!" Ginny refocused on Colin, who'd grabbed the first aid kit from the back wall and now worked to stem the blood flow from Mrs. McCall's head wound. "Colin, what can I do?"

Colin glanced back at her and her heart constricted. He stayed so calm when all she wanted to do was scream. What would she have done without him here?

His gaze shifted over her shoulder. "Beverly, can you head outside and direct the first responders inside when they arrive?"

For the second time in less than a minute, Ginny's chest grew tight. Behind her, calm and smug as ever, stood Beverly Dorn. The woman's arms were folded across her stomach, and she regarded the injured receptionist with cool passivity. "Certainly, I will. How tragic. And here I thought it was a student playing a prank. Most unfortunate."

She left the office without another word and Ginny had to resist the urge to run after the woman and shake her by the shoulders. *Unfortunate?* That's it? A woman lay bleeding on the floor from a head wound and she called it unfortunate?

Colin still hadn't answered Ginny's question. Even Sam crouched down to assist with the receptionist as he made calls for help, phone receiver shoved between his ear and shoulder.

"Colin? I want to help. What can I do?"

Colin finished wrapping a piece of gauze around Mrs. McCall's head, checked the clock in the corner of the room and finally turned his attention back to her.

"Go. Check the lab."

Fear spiked through her skull, but she couldn't shy away from this. Would not shy away from this. She pulled on the archaeology lab's door handle, praying it remained locked. The handle turned and the door swung open. She *had* locked this. She remembered doing it not ten minutes ago.

Acid crept up the back of her throat. Black spots swam in her vision. This couldn't be happening.

The archaeology lab looked pristine, no broken pottery or scattered pages. Nothing overturned. Except…

Colin reached her side as she pointed into the room, her index finger extending toward the previously locked cupboard at the far side of the room. Its doors were wide open, shelves bare. The heavy lock lay in pieces on the floor.

"They're gone." She barely had the strength to form the words. Her knees hit the floor with a crack, but she felt nothing. Nothing but dread, terror and fear. Her life, her career was over. She couldn't help the Amarans, couldn't bring their lost history back to the people who deserved it. They'd trusted her with the tablets, and now they were gone.

Colin knelt beside her and took her hand the same way he had the day before. Gentle. Unassuming. Requiring nothing in return, offering only comfort. "Please tell me this robbery didn't just set off an international incident between the United States and the Kingdom of Amar."

Breathe, Ginny. Breathe. But she didn't want to. She wanted to sink into the floor. Make all of this disappear. "I don't… I don't…" A glimpse of the paramedics arriving to take Mrs. McCall to the hospital set her off again, each breath coming in sharp gasps.

Drowning. She was drowning on air and no one could save her.

Colin's arms wrapped around her shoulders, drawing her to his chest. He held her head against his sternum, and the pressure of his embrace eased the effort in her lungs.

She didn't know how much time passed. It could have been hours or only minutes, but eventually and all too soon, Colin released her and held her at arm's length. His jaw was chiseled stone, hard and determined. "Mrs. McCall appears critical. This is beyond unacceptable. I need to know what's on those tablets that's worth killing for."

TEN

After the police arrived, Colin connected Sam with an officer who could take the student to a sketch artist, and then gingerly helped Ginny to her feet. She continued taking deep, noisy breaths to steady herself, but she was not the kind of person who handled repeated life-or-death situations well. He didn't mind. In fact, he appreciated that her strengths lay elsewhere. Her intelligence lent her beauty an appealing softness that he found increasingly difficult to ignore.

She took small, shuffling steps as they made their way to Ginny's car, now parked closer to the school thanks to a thoughtful officer who'd noticed the professor's pale complexion and trembling limbs. While Colin didn't want to press her until she felt calmer, he had to ask a question that the Service—and the FBI, and Homeland Security—needed to know. "So, about our relationship with Amar. Are we in trouble?"

She pursed her lips before responding. "Maybe. No. We shouldn't be. It's not our fault, and other things have happened so it's not as if we had control here. They were secured as per the loan agreement, so fault can't fall on us."

"You sure both governments will see it that way?"

"They have to. Guess I'll have to cancel all the rest of my appointments with Dr. Hilden. Wait…no!" She grabbed his arm in excitement but let go just as quickly, a hint of color returning to her cheeks. "Uh, sorry. I had an idea. I might be able to find old photos from the early archaeological field reports back when the tablets were first dug up. If those reports have been archived online, I can still work on the translations even without having the tablets in my hand."

As much as Colin knew he should be excited about this for her, he couldn't muster the same enthusiasm. "We put a woman in an ambulance not an hour ago because of these tablets and the research you're doing. It might be wise to pull back and take another look at what's going on before diving back into things."

Ginny's eyebrows rose and she coughed in disbelief. "Aren't you the one who told me not to listen to these people? That I shouldn't give in to their demands?"

"Yes, but that was before someone got driven off to the hospital in critical condition."

"What about what happened with Donna?"

Colin sighed and gestured back toward the Daviau Center, where police officers filtered in and out as they tried to make sense of the attack. "Look around, Ginny. Then tell me if you think it's a good idea to continue working on this while there are innocent lives at stake. I know I said it's not the nature of my training or of the Secret Service to discourage protect-ees from going about their work, but some-one is going to a lot of trouble to make sure you don't work on your translations. Until we know exactly why, all I'm suggesting is that we take a step back and try to gain some per-spective. Maybe take a harder look at what you already have."

She took another deep breath and exhaled slowly. "You're right, but there are also more lives here to think about than only the people we see in front of us. This work could benefit so many people—an entire country and our knowledge of human history, for starters—so if someone wants it stopped, there must be something massive at stake. We need to look at all the angles."

Colin agreed with her, but right now not knowing the nature of that something was exactly the problem. "From here on out, no more assumptions. Every move we make has to be fully deliberate." He opened the car door for her and waited as she climbed inside.

"Do you think whoever is after my work will actually try something else at this point?" She leaned her head against the glass as Colin secured himself in the driver's seat. "I mean, they have the physical tablets, so they may think they've done enough and leave me alone. Especially if I pull back from my work for a little while."

He heard the bitterness in her voice. "I'm not asking you to sabotage your future, Ginny. The thing is, in my experience these kinds of enemies don't always think along sensible lines. After this attack, I have no doubt Chief Black will devote plenty of additional resources to investigating the incidents. I hate to say it, but that might put an even greater target on your back."

"But if we figure out what's going on and what it is that's valuable about my research?"

"That'd help."

Ginny grew silent again as he drove. When he pulled into the motel parking lot, she sat upright and tapped on the car's digital clock. "Colin, the second drop!"

He'd hoped she might forget about that. "The police are going to monitor the drop site. I want you far away from there today. If you're ready to go back tomorrow, fine, but like I said, think carefully about this."

He put the car in Park and jogged around to open the passenger side door for Ginny. A battle played out across her features. Hopefully she'd be able to rest today and gain some perspective for the days ahead. "Let me check the room before you head inside." A quick sweep of the motel suite revealed nothing untoward.

"Thanks. For taking care of me." She paused in the doorway and turned to face him. "You've got to be exhausted, too. Maybe ask for several officers to spell you tonight, okay? I don't want to wake up tomorrow to find you passed out in the car."

He smirked, though she wasn't far off the mark. He could go full throttle for weeks under sleep deprivation thanks to training, but it was never ideal and always a risk. "Don't worry about me. Rest up and I'll keep you in the loop if any details come through, all right?"

She nodded, about to close the door, when she stopped again. Her expression changed, softened. Colin's heart did a strange flip as she regarded him under long, lacy eyelashes.

"Also, I'm sorry for how I snapped at you earlier today. In the office. It wasn't fair to you and it was rude of me not to give you the benefit of the doubt. Or a chance to defend yourself. I don't know what came over me."

Colin swallowed hard. Someone could have knocked him over with a feather. "No apology necessary. We're both under a lot of pressure."

"No, no. Don't make my cruel remark less than it was. The thing is—" she took a deep breath before continuing "—I've had some bad experiences with relationships. Related to my appearance."

He had a sudden urge to find all those men and teach them a lesson or two about respecting women. "Ginny, you're the most beautiful and capable woman I've ever met. I realize the, uh…your scar is a part of you and a part of your past, and I'm sorry you had to go through whatever put it there. Please know it was never my intention to make you feel unlovely or less than you are." A light-headedness overcame him as the words he spoke brought to light a realization. He was falling for Virginia Anderson, against all logic, reason and experience.

"I know, and I suppose my experiences

have made me more sensitive and too quick to react."

"We all have scars, Ginny." Why was he still speaking? Why couldn't he just say good-night and walk away? "Every single one of us. Just because some of our scars aren't visible on the outside doesn't mean they're not as painful or horrific or that we don't also struggle to live with them each and every day. But you know what? The important thing, the most important thing in this life, is that we learn how to live with our scars. How to appreciate them and what they've taught us."

She regarded him thoughtfully, and though her eyes had grown red and wet with emotion, she still smiled. Soft and inviting. "And what God will teach us through them and because of them. Even though it hurts sometimes."

And then his hand was on her cheek. Touching her scarred skin. He pulled his hand away, suddenly so aware of her presence, her scent and the surprise in her eyes that had to reflect his own.

"Colin—"

But her words went no further because his mouth covered hers, banishing the distance between them. Sweet as honey and gentle as the autumn breeze, Colin felt Ginny relax into the kiss, the tension in her shoulders melting away as they claimed this moment as their own.

Until she pressed her hands against Colin's chest and pushed, severing the moment.

"I'm sorry," she said. "I can't." She backed into the motel room and slammed the door.

Colin's heart nearly split in two. How had she wormed her way into his affections so deeply in only a few days? And why did he get the sense that the feeling was mutual...and that it terrified them both?

ELEVEN

Ginny endured a night of fitful sleep, unable to shake the look on Colin's face when she'd pushed him away. But she'd had no choice. *You'll never find love*, her mother's voice echoed. *Not with a face like that.* An injured, scarred Ginny was no longer valuable to the world—or at least, the world her mother had expected her daughter to be a part of—which was why Ginny had turned to school and become a professor. If she'd amount to nothing without perfect looks, then she'd work by herself in dingy libraries and lonely classrooms where she could prove herself without being seen.

Colin could never understand the repeated heartbreak she'd endured at the other side of the table from seemingly well-meaning suitors.

On the other hand, Colin had touched her skin without flinching, seen both sides of her visage, and had kissed her anyway. *It's only a matter of time*, her mother's voice still scolded.

Whether that was true or not, Colin was a good man. Brave, honorable and a physical marvel of strength. And attractiveness. He deserved someone better. She wasn't good enough for him, and it took only one look at her ruined skin to know that to be the truth.

He was wrong. Not everyone was scarred, because some people healed. Not her.

The fifth time her snooze alarm blared, Ginny woke with sweat coating her body, her mind racing between the moment with Colin, the missing tablets and the image of Mrs. Mc-Call lying facedown with blood matting the back of her skull. A knock came at the door and she slipped off the side of the lumpy motel mattress with a shout of alarm.

"Ginny? Are you all right?" The pounding intensified as Colin's voice brought her back to reality.

"Just woke up," she replied. "I'll be out in fifteen."

Showered and dressed, she opened the door to find Colin leaning against the hood of her hatchback and sipping a large take-out cup of coffee. A second coffee sat on the roof on the passenger side. He waved to a police car across the street, which drove off after the officer behind the wheel returned the wave.

"For me?" she asked, pointing at the coffee.

His lopsided smile set her cheeks ablaze. "Of course it is. It's one perk of making friends with the local PD. They can drop off breakfast on the way by."

"We should really go get your car back from outside my apartment."

He shrugged. "If there's time. It doesn't make a big difference either way, since we should continue to travel together. I don't want anyone targeting your vehicle while you're alone inside it."

She took a sip from the takeaway cup and hissed as the liquid scalded her tongue. Colin climbed into the driver's seat without another word and they headed over to the school. From the corner of her eye, she noticed that her little travel Bible—which she normally kept in the glove box—was now wedged between the front seats. *Interesting.*

"Did you decide what you're going to do about your work?"

She didn't miss the tension in his question, and he wasn't going to like her answer. "I'm going to trust that you and the police can protect me while I do my work." He didn't respond, so she continued. "It's not every day that a person who's as low on the academic totem pole as me gets the opportunity to work with a consultant on a major project. Plus, despite my reservations about Dr. Hilden's necessity to my work, the man did travel all the way here. And let's not forget, these tablets I've been entrusted to keep safe for study do belong to his country."

"The ancient tablets that are, as of now, missing."

She winced at the verbal reminder. Certainly Dr. Hilden had been informed of the theft, but that wasn't going to make facing him this afternoon at their meeting any easier. As they reached the college and she got to work, this grew even truer with each passing hour. The bright yellow police tape around Mrs. McCall's desk didn't help her to concentrate, nor did having the severe-faced Colin hovering so close after last night's interrupted kiss.

When it came time for Colin to escort her to the library, Ginny trembled with anxiety. As usual, Dr. Hilden was already waiting in the library meeting room when Ginny arrived. He sat with his back straight, hands folded on the table. He wore the same brown tweed suit he'd been wearing the day she met him, but without the Panama hat.

"I'd begun to doubt if you were coming

today, after yesterday's cancellation," he said in his inflected English. "When I didn't receive a return call, I'd hoped that meant, as you say, no news is good news?"

"I'm so sorry." Ginny cleared her throat and set a folder down on the table. "I realize that without the tablets, it's going to be harder to get work done, but I think we can manage." Inside the folder were photographs of the tablets, which she spread across the table as Dr. Hilden leaned forward to study them. "Were you able to reach your contact in the Amaran government to explain the situation?"

"So they have not been found?" Dr. Hilden's tone turned dark. "You were entrusted with my peoples' history and you lost it to the clutches of common criminals?"

Blood rushed to her ears as she grasped for words. "I followed the lending agreement to the utmost detail."

"And you?" Dr. Hilden rounded on Colin. "What kind of a place are you running around here? Are the police so incompetent that they cannot figure out the simplest of crimes? Theft from an academic institution in broad daylight! How could you allow this to happen?"

Dr. Hilden's voice had risen to a yell, attracting the attention of students and staff walking past the meeting room. Ginny thought she might bring back up the scant coffee and doughnut she'd eaten today.

To her relief, Colin responded with absolute calm. "I assure you that the authorities are doing everything they can to retrieve the tablets and locate the persons responsible."

"The people of Amar trusted this woman."

"And she adhered one hundred percent to the guidelines of your agreement." Colin glanced at Ginny. She offered a grateful nod. He might be playing her protector, but he didn't need to go to bat for her over protocol. It surprised her that he'd so vehemently stick up for her, especially after how she'd rejected his kiss. No, *their* kiss. She'd willingly participated until reality reared its ugly head.

Dr. Hilden scowled at Colin as Ginny cleared her throat and tapped on the photos she'd set out on the table. "I think it might be best if we get working." Any more tension in the air and something was bound to snap. "I was able to retrieve the archaeological dig report photos from an online archive."

Colin picked up a photo and squinted at it. "Why don't you have better photos if these are so important?"

Ginny shook her head, familiar with questions like that from students. "The photos were taken right after the tablets were found back in the 1950s, and since they're part of a larger collection that's just been sitting inside crates in the basement of the Ashmore Museum waiting to be studied, no one has bothered to take higher-quality photographs yet. It's been unnecessary until now. Dr. Hilden and I were planning to take new ones in a professional environment so that I could have images accompanying my report. Though, we did take an initial set of condition photos back at the museum before the tablets were handed over."

"Like photographs of a rental car after you get it and before you turn it in," Colin said. "I get that."

"But they're focused on condition and not on the inscriptions themselves, so it'll be a challenge to work with them. But we could retrieve the images from Curator Wehbe in a pinch."

Dr. Hilden grunted and tapped a photo. "Good. This image is terrible. The symbols are barely legible."

Ginny rotated the photo to look at it and raised her eyebrows at the image he'd selected. "Good thing we've already translated this one, then. The degradation in image quality is what happens when creating a digital archive. The dig report from the 1950s would have needed to be scanned in. Many of these archives were created with inferior copy-and-scan technology in the nineties."

Dr. Hilden gave a terse nod and folded his arms across his chest. "Yes, yes. Of course. I meant only for comparative purposes with the other tablets' contents. Naturally."

Ginny gritted her teeth at the condescension in his tone. "Right. Except that...you know what, never mind. I think it's more important that we start with—"

Shelby, her student who worked part-time in the library, burst into the room with a look of alarm on her young face.

"Mr. Tapping? There's an urgent call for you to head back to the Criminology Department."

"What about?" Colin said with exasperation.

Shelby glanced from Ginny to Dr. Hilden before responding. "It's urgent and confidential, Professor. All I know is it has to do with the events of Tuesday night. They've found something."

It pained Colin to see the panicked look in Ginny's eyes. He knew how important this meeting was to her, and he'd already monopolized plenty of precious time with the consultant. However, leaving her alone—especially after yesterday's near-fatal attack on the receptionist—would be far too great a risk.

"We'll come back afterward," he reassured her. "Apologies, Doc. I'll bring her back as fast as I can."

As they neared the building that housed the Criminology Department, he noticed with surprise that Ginny had begun shivering in the cool autumn air. She'd left her coat behind in the library in her rush to follow him.

"Hang on. Stop for a sec." He unbuttoned his long-sleeved shirt and slipped it off, holding it out to her. He'd be fine in his T-shirt for a few minutes outside, but she looked as if she needed warmth immediately. "Sorry again. I know this isn't ideal for either of us."

Or for his heart, though it was getting more and more difficult to convince himself of the fact. Especially after last night.

"It's all right." Ginny shivered but shook her head at his offered shirt. "I guess I want to know what they've found as much as you do. And I'll be fine once we get inside. Put your shirt on before you catch cold."

The department head, Dr. Thompson, leaned out of his office to wave Colin inside as they entered the Criminology Department.

Colin slowed his steps to finish rebuttoning his shirt before Ginny followed him into the office. Thompson closed the door. Another man sat inside the office in a full army uniform, including combat boots and camouflage. He nodded at Colin as he entered.

"What's she doing here?" Thompson barked, seeing Ginny enter the room.

"Professor Anderson is as much a part of the week's events as I am, if not more," Colin stated. "Either she stays or we all go down to the police station to do this where I can see her through glass to ensure her safety while we talk. After which I'll fill her in the moment you leave the station. Your choice."

Dr. Thompson glowered but relented. "Fine. Know that I'm only letting you in on this, Tapping, due to your professional history. I know you've been working with the local police as well, and I'd like you to continue as an official liaison between the college and the police in this matter. I'm bringing this to you first for PR reasons."

Colin nodded and glanced back at Ginny, who sat quietly at the back of the room. "Go on."

The man in military uniform spoke up, a Southern Texas drawl underlying his stern and serious delivery. "As you're aware, the stun grenade used on the property several nights ago has been confirmed as military issue, an M84. What we did not know until this morning was that the grenade's origins were not off campus as originally believed."

Colin blinked at the two men. "Come again?"

"What Major Nelson is trying to say, Mr. Tapping, is that the grenade wasn't brought on property from somewhere else to be used during the library attack. It was already here."

Colin jumped up from his seat. "On property? We had a grenade on campus and nobody thought that might be a bad idea?" He looked over at Ginny, whose eyes were wide. Her complexion had paled and she regarded him with worry.

"It was meant to be part of a class presentation," Major Nelson said. "I had several pieces of nonlethal and less-than-lethal military equipment transported to the campus and secured last Sunday when very few students or staff were around to witness the transfer. The college approved the plans and assisted in securing the items until my presentation, which was to happen in—" he checked his watch "—about ten minutes."

Dr. Thompson pounded a fist on his desk. The man was flustered and Colin didn't blame him. Thompson might lose his job over this, or at least receive a suspension. "It was secure, Tapping. We had permits, extra security. The military's security guys checked it, our guys checked it. No one else knew it was there."

"Clearly, someone did," Ginny's voice chimed in. "Everything that's happened so far indicates a level of familiarity with the school."

Colin agreed. "Or the ability to obtain information without arousing suspicion."

Dr. Thompson and Major Nelson's expressions became even more perturbed than they'd been a few minutes prior. Thompson narrowed his eyes at Colin. "You think the attacks are an inside job?"

Colin shrugged, thinking of Sam and his cluelessness over leaving the reception desk near Ginny's office unattended, resulting in the department keys being ripe for the picking. "Not necessarily. All this would take is one smart, attentive individual. And we already are fairly certain he has lackeys—a hired crew doing some of the more technology-dependent legwork. The police are working on identifying one of the perps after yesterday's events. I'm afraid it could be anyone, gentlemen. Maybe someone you've never met or never noticed before. Or it could be the result of loose lips from somebody who might not even know they're being used as eyes and ears."

Or a randomly appearing military man who'd found a way to legitimately bring a grenade onto campus and then claim its disappearance? Colin didn't voice this thought, but the whole situation didn't sit right.

Thompson groaned and pounded his fist on his desk again. "This is going to be a PR nightmare if anyone outside this office gets wind of it."

Colin exchanged looks with Ginny. He knew she'd keep quiet, and whom would he tell other than Chief Black? "You fill out the necessary paperwork to make a report," Colin suggested. "If you *just* discovered the missing grenade, I assume that means it still has to be confirmed as the same one tossed by Tuesday night's assailant. We'll deal with that when the time comes. For now, sit tight."

He rose and exited, leaving a stunned but resigned Dr. Thompson and Major Nelson behind. He didn't turn around until he'd left the building and reached the quad.

Ginny stood behind him, uncertainty written across her lovely features.

"So, now what?" She crossed her arms, once again shivering in the cold.

He sighed and rubbed his eye with the heel of his hand. He needed sleep. "We'll head back to the library so you can finish your meeting. But let's be more careful about whom we talk to concerning what's going on. If this is an inside job or if someone on campus is being played as a patsy, we don't want to scare them into doing something drastic. Not yet, anyway. You're still too vulnerable and we still don't have enough information. Actually, we should take a quick drive to the police station before heading back to Hilden, okay? They need to know what we just learned."

She dropped her arms as a slight breeze kicked up and blew her windswept hair off her cheek for half a second, revealing the perceived imperfection that he suspected had something to do with her abrupt cancellation of the previous night's kiss. Which he was not going to think about.

No distractions. Because of a distracted heart, he hadn't been able to protect Lynn the way he'd been trained to, but he had a chance to make things right here. He could make sure no one was able to hurt Ginny. Not again, not ever.

Forget Ginny's "God is in control" assertions. This time, he wanted to be the one in control, lest Ginny pay for his lack of perfect control with her life.

TWELVE

Colin paced back and forth in front of the library meeting room where Ginny and Dr. Hilden worked feverishly on the tablet translations. They needed to get the work done as fast and as accurately as possible—Colin saw that now—because it very well could provide the greatest clue as to the reason behind these attacks and why the tablets had been stolen.

Dr. Hilden hadn't been all that impressed by Colin's assertion that he and Ginny needed to work on the report as long as possible today, but while the man's obvious superiority complex rubbed him the wrong way, Colin chalked it up to the stress of the situation. Dr. Hilden couldn't be having an easy time of it, trying to explain to Amar's government that its ancient artifacts had disappeared on the other side of the world while he was supposed to be looking out for them.

Here in the United States, an incident like

that—even though it hadn't been the man's fault that they'd been stolen, or Ginny's for that matter—would get a person stripped of his or her job position and torn apart in the media. So far, Colin hadn't seen any local or national news about it, which meant the police and the college were doing a good job of keeping things under wraps.

On the other hand, a lack of public awareness meant the local police hadn't received any outside leads. Chief Black had called to let Colin know they'd immediately begun some internal questioning of college staff to try to piece together the break-in and disappearance of the stun grenade, but Colin had a theory that the investigation would do nothing beyond reveal where the college lacked in general security—such as not having cameras trained on important closets, no matter how tightly locked down anyone believed them to be. As for Sam's description to the sketch artist, the person who'd told him about Ginny's car being towed had actually been another student. The police had located the student and were interrogating him about the situation, which Chief Black believed would result in yet another sketch being taken. It meant more time wasted, which they didn't have.

As he paced, Colin scoured online auction

sites for evidence of the tablets on the black market. When he came up empty, he resorted to calling every major museum in the country to warn them against anyone trying to sell ancient Amaran tablets without paperwork.

They said goodbye to Dr. Hilden around nine o'clock, and Colin took a barely coherent, half-asleep Ginny back to the motel so she could rest. He'd suspected she would want to continue working on the translations through the weekend, but he hadn't expected to be awakened at a quarter to seven in the morning by a rap on the car window. He awoke from a restless sleep to see Ginny and the officer who'd spelled him for a few hours standing outside the car. The officer gave an apologetic shrug when Colin shot him a questioning glance.

"Rise and shine, Mr. Tapping," Ginny quipped, coming around to the passenger side door. He unlocked it so she could climb in.

"Decided to get an early start, did you?" Colin tried to shake off the grogginess. Maybe he'd been more sleep deprived than he'd realized. "What do you have there?"

"Peace offering." Ginny held up a brown paper bag and a takeaway coffee cup.

He took it and peered inside, unable to suppress a grin. "Is this a blueberry fritter?"

She extended the cup to him. "And I thought

you might need this, too. It was my turn to call in a breakfast order. And I know you've said you're used to this kind of watching or protecting, but it can't be easy. You really do look exhausted."

"Thanks."

"No, Colin, I mean... I appreciate it. I do. I know I probably haven't been the easiest protectee so far, but I think I'm starting to get it." She paused as though she had something else to say, but the words stalled on her tongue. Colin didn't mind, and he didn't want to push her. Still, he didn't try to suppress his smile.

He set the coffee down in the cup holder between the seats and pulled the fritter out of the paper bag. He took a bite that spilled flakes of sugary glaze all over the driver's seat, surprised at his own physical hunger. When had he last eaten a proper meal? It wouldn't be the first time he'd become so wrapped up in a protective detail that he'd forgotten to eat. "Then I guess I should thank you for noticing."

Ginny pursed her lips, brushed a lock of hair behind her ear—uncovering her smooth cheek, he noticed—and crossed her arms over her stomach. "You're welcome."

An awkward silence descended as neither of them spoke. He polished off the doughnut and began the drive to the college, assuming that was where she wanted to go. They passed no students on campus on the way to Ginny's office, but what student would be voluntarily awake at seven in the morning on a Saturday?

Colin felt tempted to relax, to let down his guard. It was a false sense of security, he knew, and too similar to the day he'd let his heart run away—and made the mistake that cost a woman her life.

"Did you make much progress last night on the translations?"

As they reached her office, Ginny unlocked her door and set her bag inside, then turned back to him as her uncertain smile morphed into a joyous grin. "We did. And I know, maybe I shouldn't have, but I woke up at two o'clock and kept going. You're not going to believe this, but I was able to translate all but two, which then allowed me to write and submit a first-draft version of my report to Dr. Hilden and Curator Wehbe for review. I sent it over at six thirty this morning, and I'm hoping we can meet Monday afternoon to finalize the report. We'll publish it in a few peer-reviewed journals next month. Colin, I think I've found the—"

A bang and a shower of glass stopped Ginny midsentence as her window exploded inward. A large satchel covered in flames flew through the window and landed with a thump inside the office. Ginny jumped back in surprise and batted at her leg to smother the tiny tongue of flame caught at the hem of her pants. Colin reacted on instinct, crossing the office in a flash and pulling her out of the doorway.

He rushed down the hall to grab the emergency fire extinguisher, then ran back. Ginny had opened up her water bottle and was trying to toss the water at the burning satchel. Pops and bangs from inside the bag sent his nerves into a frenzy.

"Step back," he shouted before letting the extinguisher's foam spray all over the satchel and the floor. Within seconds, the fire was out. "You okay?"

Ginny nodded and raced over to the broken window, but Colin grabbed her arm and yanked her back. If someone was watching, she'd be too easily exposed.

The room grew silent, their breath the only sound. He looked down at Ginny since she hadn't yet answered him, only to find their faces so very, very close together. Eyes locked, lips parted.

And then Ginny's eyes focused behind him and she cried out, pulling away. She stared down at the foamy, charred lump, then knelt, brushing foam off the blackened satchel. She opened it and reached inside. "No, no, no, no…"

Colin knelt next to her, his heart racing at the panic and agony in her voice. "Are those what I think they are?"

She lifted out a handful of crumbled, broken clay. Her hand shook, the tremor extending up her arm and into her whole body. "They're gone. Destroyed. I can't believe it. Thousands of years of history."

Colin reached inside the bag and pulled out a clip and a piece of bullet casing. "And that same someone had a really stupid idea to try to kill or injure you in the process. Bullets in a fire. Good myth, but it only works in movies."

Ginny's complexion paled. "What did they think, that the bullets would go off and hit us when they exited the bag?"

"Probably. But they put the bullets inside this leather bag, and the fire didn't get hot enough to set off more than a few of these things. They're only .20 caliber. Not enough to do much more than give you a bad scratch from the brass casing. Maybe poke your eye out if you had your head stuck in the bag." He sat back on his heels and rolled the casing between his fingers.

Ginny sighed, her breath shaky and full of emotion. Her eyes were still trained on the decimated contents of the bag at her feet. "With the tablets stolen, I'd hoped maybe this would end…but I suppose it was too much to ask."

Colin wanted to shout with frustration at the arrogance of such an attack. The first attack in the library had been the military-issue stun grenade, a less-than-lethal professional piece of equipment that someone obviously knew how to use to maximum effectiveness, but bullets inside a bag on fire? He had no doubt that this was intended to be a two-pronged attack. If the bullets didn't kill Ginny—if they'd only injured her—the destroyed tablets had to be a contingency plan to shake her to the core, a punishment for not following through on the second drop. Making this attack the morning after she'd made a breakthrough could not be a coincidence.

To steal the tablets, then return them in pieces? Their opponent knew very well what this would do to Ginny's confidence and how devastating this would be on the chance that the bullets didn't kill her outright. The person after her work was willing to destroy every piece of her, bit by bit, tearing her down physically and mentally until she was worn down to nothing. Their enemy knew how to get inside her head, tear her down from the inside out.

Doubtless their enemy had hoped Colin would be killed or injured at the same time.

"Someone saw us come in this building. They knew we were in this office." But he hadn't seen anyone on their way inside. It only served to reinforce his growing sense of concern about being here on a quiet day with few people about.

"But I didn't tell anyone." She paused, recall drawing across her features. "Last night, after getting back to the motel, I had an urgent email from the dean about a meeting I'd missed yesterday regarding the tenure-track position requirements. I had to message him back about working with Dr. Hilden and may have mentioned being close to a breakthrough. And that I'd be here sometime today if we could reschedule. Oh, no."

He tensed. "Who else knows, Ginny?"

"Beverly Dorn. She was CC'd as part of the discussion, since we're both competing for the same position." She swallowed hard, staring at the satchel of destroyed tablets.

"No one else?"

Ginny thought for a moment. "Donna. I sent Donna a private message over social media this morning. I was just so excited."

Beverly Dorn, Donna, the Dean, the curator who'd loaned her the tablets in the first place, as well as the Amaran representative. The only ones who knew she'd be here. It didn't make sense. None of those people had any motive to harm Ginny or want her research stopped, except for maybe Beverly Dorn. He couldn't dismiss the woman's coldness upon discovering Mrs. McCall's injured form lying on the floor, but was she the type to toss grenades and write threatening letters?

"Call the museum," Colin said, thinking out loud. "Get your meeting moved to this afternoon. Or first thing when they open, if you can."

"This morning? Why?"

"Whoever wanted you to stop your work may have thought they'd succeeded after stealing the tablets. Now that you've made a breakthrough, it seems like that's the one thing they were afraid of. They want you to know that they can destroy your life's work or, if possible, simply eliminate you from the picture outright before you can tell anyone in person what you've learned. Someone just tried to kill you, Ginny. They failed, but the fact is, all other attempts up to this point haven't been specifically designed to kill you in particular, only injure or frighten. Do your translations contain anything that could be a motive for murder?"

"I don't see how."

"Then we need to dig harder to figure it out. These pieces need connecting today, because I have a feeling whoever is after you is not going to stop just because this attempt didn't succeed."

Ginny choked back tears as she gathered up her bags. Colin hustled them both out of the office, a worried look in his eyes. She said nothing, but had a good idea what bothered him. If someone had just tried to kill her, might the person come looking for the body? And what would happen when the attacker didn't find it?

The satchel of destroyed tablets felt like an anvil, weighing down her hopes, her future, ready to sink it all to the bottom of the ocean. How could this have happened? What kind of a callous monster would destroy pieces of history? She thanked God once again for Colin's presence. She'd been wrong to resent him. The man knew what he was doing, and if she'd been left to deal with the satchel of destroyed tablets on her own, she'd have crumbled into a million tiny pieces, too.

She couldn't wrap her mind around it. Why would someone try to kill her over a few translated sentences? She hadn't definitively proved that the summer palace was buried in the area she suspected—that would be the archaeological team's job, providing a group could get funding to dig in that location—and even if it was there, what value could there possibly be in preventing her from telling someone about it?

After a shaky and tear-filled phone call to the curator, at 9 a.m. they made their way to the museum. She had to face the music one way or another, historical breakthrough or not.

"Professor Anderson, welcome." Curator Wehbe interrupted her thoughts, approaching from the museum's front atrium. "Let us meet in my office. Will sir be joining us?"

"He will," Colin said, reaching across and shaking the curator's hand. "Don't worry, I won't get in the way. Just here in an observational capacity." He scanned the museum entrance, completely void of visitors. "Quiet morning."

Mr. Wehbe flicked his hand at the front door. "Saturday mornings usually are. We have several community groups coming through later and I assure you, it won't be quiet once they arrive. Please, right this way."

They entered the curator's office, where Dr. Hilden waited. Photographs spread across the table showed off the now-decimated tablets in their whole form. Dr. Hilden paged through a packet of papers, a frown on his wide face. Ginny's insides tightened.

"Professor Anderson," he said without looking up, "the curator filled me in regarding the disturbing news about the tablets. Is it true that they've been destroyed?"

Ginny sat, swallowing the lump in her throat that had been there since the moment she'd held the crumbled clay in her hands. "Yes. They're gone. I hadn't expected them to be returned to us anytime soon, but I'd rather they hadn't shown up at all than for them to be returned in pieces."

"And you believe that whoever destroyed them, their intent was malicious?"

Ginny almost laughed at the ludicrous question. "I can't see how it could be construed otherwise. They were tossed into my office through the window. With the bag on fire. And there were bullets inside."

"What?" Mr. Wehbe blinked rapidly. "You could have been killed!"

"Not exactly, but it appears that was part of the intention," Colin said. "The rest of it was pure arrogance. There was no need to destroy the artifacts, but someone who believes they're going to get away with everything would likely see it as one more blow to Ginny's research and a way to get inside her head, shake her up even more and force her to back off in the event that the bullets didn't kill her. Without the stolen tablets in our enemy's hands, we have no real way of tracing the theft, either." He held his hands up when Mr. Wehbe and Dr. Hilden looked his way. "Sorry. Staying out of it now."

Ginny took a deep breath and plunged forward. "I understand we'll have to take extreme care in how we explain this to Amar, but we have the dig site photographs and my report. I have hope that this is not a complete loss. If we get one or two peers to agree with my supposition, I think we can apply for a dig permit for the site. We might even be able to send a team over by the end of the year. Perhaps over Christmas break."

"Wonderful," the curator said, clapping his hands together. Relief washed over Ginny. Her relief lasted only a moment, until she saw the scowl on Dr. Hilden's face.

"So soon?" Dr. Hilden set down the stack of papers he'd been paging through and crossed his arms. "Dig permits. A bit premature, don't you think?"

Mr. Wehbe tut-tutted. "Not at all, and certainly not impossible with your support and advocacy with the Amaran government. If she can obtain validation and additional support from several peers—"

"She hasn't proven anything."

"You've got to be joking," Mr. Wehbe said as Ginny's heart began to sink. "We're here to discuss her report on these tablets, the report you've been helping her put together thus far. You've given no indication that you don't support her theories on the summer palace's location."

"Her translations are incorrect. This paper cannot be published as it stands."

His words sliced like a sword to the gut. How could Dr. Hilden say that? He'd helped with and encouraged her work all week and had shown nothing but enthusiasm this whole time. They'd worked so hard all of yesterday afternoon and evening so that she could prepare this paper over the weekend. "I don't understand."

"It's a ridiculous assertion. It cannot be published and the Amaran government will not support it."

"I've already submitted my abstracts outlining the theory to several prominent publications." Ginny glanced over her shoulder at Colin, whose impassive gaze had narrowed in on the Amaran representative. "I'm not here for permission to publish, I thought this meeting was to refine my thesis and argument within the paper."

Dr. Hilden swept a hand across the table and scooped up the photographs of the tablets. He collected them into a pile and, before Ginny realized his intentions, tore them down the middle. And then into quarters.

"No!" Ginny lunged across the table to try to grab the pieces, but Dr. Hilden tucked the torn bits into his coat pocket and stood.

"Retract your abstracts. I will be returning to Amar this afternoon. Thank you for your cooperation, Mr. Wehbe, Professor Anderson, but I'm afraid that my time is better spent elsewhere. Good day." He walked around the table and headed to the door. Ginny stared after him in disbelief. Behind her, Mr. Wehbe sputtered in confusion.

Before the man could exit the room, Colin's hand shot out and grasped Dr. Hilden's arm. "Who purchased the land?" he asked, his impassive expression unchanged.

"Excuse me?" Dr. Hilden's cheeks grew pink at the question. "What are you on about?"

"The land that Miss Anderson thinks the summer palace might be buried on. It was recently sold. Who bought it?"

Dr. Hilden shook his head and wrenched his

arm from Colin's grasp. "How should I know? I'm no soothsayer."

"But you work for the government," Ginny said, rising from her chair. It was as if she saw this whole thing happening through a foggy lens. "And as a government representative on this project, surely you've been informed regarding the fate of the land relevant to this work."

"That's where you're mistaken, Miss Anderson."

"I don't believe you," Colin snarled.

Ginny stepped between Colin and Dr. Hilden. This wasn't supposed to be how it happened. Why had Dr. Hilden changed his mind? "What I think we're trying to understand is what changed your opinion of our research. If it's coming from outside pressures, that's fine, but it would help us to determine where to go from here. As I know you understand, this is a very important project. For Amar, for myself and for history as a whole. Surely you want what's best for the country and its people."

But Dr. Hilden only shook his head, glared past Ginny at Colin and walked out of the room.

Behind her, Ginny felt Colin lunge forward, but she stepped a few inches to the left to stop him. She blinked back the tears that came from shock. This was no time for an emotional reaction. Only logic would determine what had just happened here.

"Mr. Wehbe, do you think you could call your contact at the Ashmore Museum? See if they know whom you should contact about Dr. Hilden's visit to us? Maybe we can get through to someone in Amar's government or even at the university there. They might have an idea as to why Hilden would change his mind so quickly. There's got to be some explanation for this."

Colin tapped his foot on the floor and crossed his arms tightly over his chest. "I'd hazard a guess that it has something to do with that land sale. Maybe it was finalized and he's upset about it. Maybe access to the land has been denied somehow."

"Not if the summer palace is there. There are policies in place that give finds of historical value precedence over any other use of the land, at least until the area's been dug and a full report has been given. Amar and its policies have always cooperated with UNESCO's world heritage protection efforts in that regard."

Colin grumbled something about trying to get international organizations to cooperate with anything, but Ginny stopped paying attention when she noticed the camera on the other side of the room.

"Mr. Wehbe, can I use your computer? We loaded the condition-verifying set of digital photos of the tablets onto your computer after taking them, did we not?"

Mr. Wehbe stood, pulling a set of keys from his desk drawer. The museum curator's computer was kept in a separate locked room from his main office, for the sole purpose of giving off the impression that the whole museum was, in a nutshell, a piece of history. Having a piece of modern technology sitting in the office tended to discourage the atmosphere of days long past.

Ginny followed the curator into the computer nook, which was about the size of a large supply closet. Several ceramic jugs with tags were lined up along high shelves, and paintings sat with their backs facing out so as to not risk damage to their surfaces. Museum curatorship was a more difficult and arduous job than most people gave it credit for, and she didn't envy Mr. Wehbe's work one bit.

He woke up the computer and clicked around, opening and closing files. After several minutes, he dropped his hand from the mouse. "How strange. I can't find them."

"Check the trash," Colin suggested, leaning against the entrance to the computer nook. "See if it's recently been emptied."

The curator did so and looked back over his shoulder at Colin. "Twelve hours ago. Before we closed for the evening last night."

Ginny closed her eyes and took a deep breath. "Who has access to this computer?"

"Only myself and one or two members of my staff, but they have no interest in this project."

"What about the memory card in the camera? Did you clear it?" Colin stepped out into the main office and picked up the camera. He slid the memory card out of the slot and handed it to the curator. "If you didn't back it up in another way—which you should have, and we'll talk about that later—maybe the images are still on here. I'd think someone getting rid of the images would have also stolen the memory card instead of leaving it here for us, but maybe they were in a hurry and didn't see the camera in the corner."

The curator inserted the memory card into a card reader plugged into the computer. Within a few minutes, Ginny's stomachache began to subside. The images were still there.

"Let's back these up," she suggested, taking over as the curator slid aside. "And then lock up the memory card somewhere safe, just in case."

It didn't take long before the three of them were back in the office, the memory card safely locked away and a set of the images backed up in several places. It was a relief to know the history of the tablets hadn't been completely lost, but Ginny still couldn't fathom how the curator and Dr. Hilden were going to explain this to the international community.

"I hate to be the pessimist here," Colin said, breaking through Ginny's worries, "but we still have someone on the loose who clearly has an agenda not to see Ginny's theories brought to light. Based on Dr. Hilden's reaction when we came in here to discuss her work, I'd say that whoever is behind these attacks and the tablet destruction has also gotten to the Kingdom of Amar's government. They're running scared. We need to figure out what's happening so we know whom to go after. It may not give us all the answers, but we need someplace to start."

"You really ought to try keeping yourselves up-to-date," came a voice from the doorway. Ginny whirled around and immediately cringed, hoping her reaction hadn't been too obvious. Beverly Dorn stood in the doorway, hands folded across the front of her immaculately tailored blazer and skirt. Ginny swallowed hard at seeing the perfectly coiffed woman stride into the room with confidence. She glanced down at her own wrinkled cotton pants and purple blouse. The tiny coffee stain on the bottom of her blouse hadn't seemed like a big deal this morning, but standing next to Beverly…and why hadn't she bothered to run a brush through her hair before tossing it up in a messy half bun?

Heat rose to her cheeks as Beverly glanced at Ginny with a sidelong gaze. "Professor Anderson, tenure is not so casual a posting. I expected better from someone with your education and publishing record, though I can't say I'm disappointed. It simply paves an easier path for myself."

Ginny swallowed a rude retort that bubbled to the tip of her tongue. This woman was her colleague, no matter how frustrating or annoying she happened to be. "I've been somewhat preoccupied with other matters these days."

"Someone may have tried to kill Ginny a few hours ago," Colin added, his words clipped. "So you'll have to excuse us if we're not on top of the morning news."

"Oh! My apologies." Beverly's eyebrows lifted and dropped with feigned repentance. "I'll let you get on with it, then. Curator, I'm here for our meeting to discuss the upcoming European masters gallery exhibit."

"Yes, yes. Of course." Mr. Wehbe nodded to Ginny and Colin in turn. "You'll have to excuse us. Please do let me know of any updates. I will do my best to contact the Ashmore and to speak again with Dr. Hilden. Perhaps we can amend the relations there."

Colin left the room with a final glare over his shoulder at Beverly, but Ginny remained planted. Beverly clearly had information that Ginny didn't have and was going to make Ginny beg for it, placing her in the woman's debt for helping her out.

Pride told Ginny to get out of there and figure this out on her own, but after the events of the morning, could she really afford to let pride get the better of her? No matter how rude Dr. Dorn acted or how intimidating her appearance, there was more here at stake than personal feelings.

"Beverly," Ginny began, her stomach churning once again, "you mentioned there's been some kind of news update this morning that's relevant to my work? As I've been otherwise occupied dealing with an attempt on my life, would you mind enlightening me to lessen the blow?"

The woman's smile was smug and shameless. "Of course, Miss Anderson. The details of the land sale were released today. It's been sold to Empress Oil."

An *oil company*? The bottom dropped out of Ginny's world. Oil companies dug and drilled, and if they dug up the land before she'd had a chance to tell the world about the summer palace, it would be lost forever.

THIRTEEN

Colin followed Ginny as she stormed out of the curator's office. Confusion and fury marred her typically serene expression, and he didn't blame her. He'd verify the reports, of course, but if the land in Amar had been sold to an oil company, they had a whole other set of problems. No wonder the details of the sale had been private; there'd likely have been massive upset over that kind of a sale on potentially historic land. The offer to the Kingdom of Amar's government must have been a size it couldn't refuse. As much as it frustrated him to think Amar would accept an offer from an oil company for protected land that potentially housed a massive trove of archaeological history, he couldn't fault it for accepting an offer that would immediately benefit the country and its infrastructure.

Ginny had made some fair points on that

issue and he was beginning to see her point of view, as unfair as it seemed in the moment.

At the edge of the museum parking lot, Ginny's steps faltered. She stumbled and he lunged forward to catch her and guide her to the grassy strip between the edge of the museum driveway and the parking lot. "Take a breather, okay? There's a lot to process right now."

Her breath hitched with each inhale. He sat down next to her on the grass. She tucked her knees up to her chin and plucked at blades of grass by her feet, twining the green strips together in a loose braid. She tossed them into the soft autumn breeze. "I'm spent. I have nothing left. I'm not made for this like you are, Colin. I don't know what to do anymore."

He caught her gaze and held it, jolted by an undeniable truth. Virginia Anderson was tenacious and beautiful, intelligent and driven. He liked everything about her, and it was quickly becoming so much more than like. His affection had deepened with everything she said and did, and despite his constant efforts to shove the moment from his memory, he'd be lying if he said he hadn't been tempted to replay the moment he'd kissed her over in his mind since the moment his lips had left hers.

If only they'd met at another time, in another place, under different circumstances.

A sudden theory formed as he watched her twist more blades of grass together. Would the details of the land sale make a difference? "I want to think that this might end now. That all these attacks on you and on the tablets were designed to prevent you from finding out more about the land sale. If you'd known, you might have contacted the Amaran government with proof that the sale shouldn't go through."

She shook her head. "But I had no proof, not really. It wasn't cohesive until I put my report together. No one would stop a sale of that size without concrete evidence."

"But if your work hadn't been delayed and interrupted by everything that's happened this week, do you think you might have been able to present concrete evidence?"

"You mean put together my results and then have someone from the University of Amar head over to do an emergency survey and test pit? It might have been possible, but no guarantee."

She let the second grass braid float away on the breeze, but she looked so dejected that his arms rose on instinct, ready to draw her into a comforting hug. Instead, he pulled them back down and sat on his hands. "We should try to contact Dr. Hilden. If he's had a few minutes to cool off, you might be able to speak to him and get a more logical explanation for his reaction."

Ginny nodded. "That's a good idea. Since it doesn't look like I'm going to be getting that help for my report, I should contact the University of Amar and let them know about my findings. I don't know if it's still possible to send someone out on the land now that it's sold, but—"

The soothing tones of Vivaldi's *The Four Seasons* broke through their discussion.

"Autumn?" Colin thought he recognized the concerto, and was relieved when Ginny nodded and pulled her phone from her purse. "Ah, a ringtone. How thematically timely."

"I don't recognize the number, but I should get this." She held the phone up to her ear. "Good afternoon, Virginia Anderson speaking."

Colin watched as her face morphed from disinterest to confusion and then to shock. Her eyes flicked to his and she pulled the phone away from her ear. "Who is—?"

She put one finger to her lips and pressed a button on the screen. Immediately, the caller's voice came through on speakerphone.

"—no time for letters, Miss Anderson. You

have failed to heed my warnings, and others have paid the price. Do you care so little for your colleagues, Professor?"

The voice was muffled and distorted. The person on the other end was using a voice-altering device. Colin moved in closer to the phone to block the breeze from the speakers. When neither of them responded quickly enough, the caller continued.

"I admit I am impressed. Beyond all comprehension, you have evaded my attempts at forcing you to stop this ludicrous research. I put a great deal of thought into my gift this morning, Professor. If you won't die, the least you could do is give up."

"You tried to kill me and it failed," Ginny retorted. "And I'll never give up."

The caller chuckled, as though the act of taking a life was nothing more than a schoolyard prank. "Ah, so impulsive. Where is your logical brain now? You no longer have your precious tablets, so you are unable to physically support your theories. Your relationship with the Kingdom of Amar is tarnished and you will never gain access to the land. Your paper will be easily refuted and your reputation besmirched. Your effort to obtain tenure at the college will fail. Thus, I propose one final arrangement.

"To amend the situation you find yourself in, and to ensure you live long enough to do so, you will publish a retraction of your previous work. You will pull the submitted abstracts and destroy them. You will forget you ever saw the tablets and you will relinquish all claim on this line of work and withdraw from all contacts with Amar and its people. Do this, Miss Anderson, and I shall personally see to it that you live to see another sunrise."

As the man talked, Colin watched Ginny's face. The woman looked scared, certainly, but as the caller continued, her expression hardened. By the time the caller demanded that she relinquish all claim on her work in Amaran history, her face had turned a shade of deep pink.

"Who do you think you are?" she shouted into the phone. "You can't just demand that I give up my life's work. This discovery is important for the people of Amar. The country needs—"

Colin tapped Ginny on the shoulder, trying to signal with his other hand that she shouldn't respond to the man. The more emotional she became, the more power she gave him.

"Am I to understand," the caller interrupted, "that you refuse my offer?"

Colin signaled again that she shouldn't

speak, but the woman had a mind of her own and an anger that burned hotter than he could extinguish in the heat of the moment.

"Not only do I refuse," Ginny said, "but I'm publishing my paper *today*. Whoever you are, you won't get away with this. I'll make my findings public, and then we'll see how the international community feels about selling off land full of Amar's ancient history to be destroyed by some heartless oil company that only cares about—"

"Wrong answer."

A dial tone cut through Ginny's diatribe, and Ginny dropped the phone as though it burned her. Colin sat back on the grass, his stomach sinking into his feet.

"What just happened?" Ginny whispered. Fury abated, she regarded him with wide, frightened eyes. "Did I just..."

"You antagonized the man who hired someone to try to kill you this morning, yes."

"Oh, no. Colin, I didn't think, I reacted... He asked me to..."

"It's your life's work, and something that will change others' lives. I understand."

She launched herself across the small space of grass between them and slipped into his arms. He wrapped her in a tight hug and then released her. When she sat back on the grass, he stood and reached out to help her up.

"Thank you," she said, taking his hand. "But now what? Do you think they'll come after me again?"

Something zipped past Colin's ear and kicked up dirt next to Ginny's knee.

Colin knew instinctively what *that* was. He yanked Ginny to her feet and pulled her into the parking lot. Her vehicle sat in the same spot as it always did, but when a second bullet whizzed past his arm, he pulled Ginny behind the closest parked car.

"What is that?" Ginny cried. "Is someone shooting at us?"

"That's exactly what they're doing," Colin growled. "Keep your head down."

She crouched in front of the rear tire as Colin peeked over the hood of the vehicle. The shots had come from behind them, back toward the museum. His rapid visual scan revealed no one, so he rejoined Ginny.

"I can't see anyone. Do you have your phone?"

Ginny shook her head. "It's still in the grass. I didn't get to pick it back up when you pulled me over here."

Colin tugged his phone from his pocket and

handed it to her. "Call 911, tell them we're taking fire."

A bullet zoomed past Ginny's hands and she screamed, dropping the phone. The shot had been fired from a completely different angle. Where was it coming from?

"Forget it, let's move!" He grabbed Ginny's arm as she snatched up the phone and pulled her toward her car. "Get your keys out!"

"They're in my purse on the grass," Ginny shouted.

Gritting his teeth, Colin drew his SIG Sauer and met her eyes. "Together. On three. Stay behind me, I'll cover you." She nodded and he counted backward. "Three. Two. One. Go!"

He burst out of cover first, returning several rounds of fire toward where he surmised was the direction of the shooter based on the angle of the receiving shots. If the shooter wanted Ginny, he'd have to go through Colin first. Ginny screamed as shots hit the ground near her purse, but she grabbed the bag and they raced to seek cover at the back of her hatchback. They crouched by the vehicle as Ginny dug into her purse. She pulled out her keys, unlocked the car and tapped on the rear door. "We can crawl in through the back. The rear seats fold down, so we should be able to slide through and climb into the front."

It was a good plan, with one exception. Based on the ability of the shooter to change angles so quickly, they were dealing with someone up high—possibly on the museum roof. If there was a sniper on the roof, they could feasibly target Ginny through the car windshield, which faced the museum.

"I'll go for the driver's seat," Colin said, coming to a decision. "You'll crawl in after me but stay in the backseat, just like the other day. I'll get us out of the parking lot while you call the cops. Deal?"

Ginny hesitated only a moment. "Deal."

Colin didn't want to consider what might happen if they were dealing with more than one shooter or if he'd misjudged the angle of the shots. The moment required decisive action. He pressed the button to unlock the hatchback and slipped inside the cargo space to lower the seats. In a matter of seconds, he'd climbed into the driver's seat and started the car, praying that Ginny had climbed into the vehicle behind him.

"Are you in?" he shouted, throwing the car into gear. A glance in the rearview mirror showed Ginny pulling the rear door shut from the inside. "Leave it, let's go!"

A thud told him the door had shut. He let the car shoot forward as Ginny scrambled into the backseat. Colin banked the car sharply to the left as stuffing exploded from the passenger's seat headrest and tiny cracks spread out like webbing from the bullet-shaped holes in Ginny's windshield.

"You okay?" he called back, his heart pounding. If those bullets were from a powerful-enough rifle—

"Yes," she said, sending relief flooding through his veins. "Just get us out of here."

Ginny crouched in the backseat on the driver's side as Colin sped toward the police station. They—the mysterious *they*—had shot at her? They really did want her dead. Even the burning satchel this morning hadn't seemed like a real threat on her life, despite Colin's and the caller's assertion that it was, but having bullets whiz by her ears…that was real. She could have died in the parking lot, all because someone wanted her to stop her research.

It was so surreal, like a plot from a movie. Except in the movies, the good guy always won, and right now, her chances of making it looked slim.

Colin escorted her inside the police station when they arrived, having her sit in the waiting room while he talked to the chief. Minutes later, he returned and sat next to her. "The chief told me the guys they sent out after your call are almost there. They'll check the place out and secure the area if need be. We're going to find this guy, Ginny."

As much as she appreciated his confidence, the logic didn't fly. "We left the scene, Colin. You think the shooter stuck around after that? He probably disappeared as soon as we did. What if he followed us? He'll be out there somewhere, waiting."

Colin sighed and leaned back in the chair. "We'll find him. After all, it's—hang on, my phone is buzzing." He pulled his phone out of his pocket and glanced at the screen before answering on speakerphone. "Deputy Director? You're on speaker. Thought I was supposed to call you."

"You're going to want to hear this, Tapping."

Ginny took in Colin's expression, which had turned dark. The man obviously held on to a great deal of bitterness over what had happened with the Service.

"Go ahead," Colin said. "But make it quick. There's a shooter on the loose over here and I'd prefer to not have any more bullets heading my way in the near future."

"Then maybe this will help. How's that Dr. Hilden we spoke about a few days back?"

Ginny shrugged as Colin glanced up at her.

"Stormed out in anger this morning during a meeting, but otherwise healthy," Colin said, not even bothering to hide his exasperation. "What's this about, sir?"

"I just got a phone call, and you're not going to like it. According to my sources, Dr. Hilden's flight from Amar arrived an hour ago, and the man is presently napping in his hotel room as he had some difficulty getting in touch with his contact at the museum over there."

Ginny shook her head. "That's not possible. His sources must be wrong."

"Who's there, Tapping?"

Colin reached over to squeeze Ginny's shoulder. "I'm with the woman who's been receiving threats about her work, sir, and we both say that's impossible. She's been working with Dr. Hilden here for the past week."

"Then someone isn't who they're claiming to be," said Bennett. "Because my source has a contact with the Kingdom of Amar's embassy in Washington, and they confirm it's him. Whoever you've been interacting with this week? It's not Dr. Hilden."

FOURTEEN

The room spun as the words sank in. Not Dr. Hilden? Then whom had she been working with? The man had known all about her work, and all about Amar's history.

But he'd only been a consultant, hadn't he? At no point had he actually taken over the translations or offered anything but counter-suggestions to the points she'd made. Most of the time, she'd thought of him as a glorified babysitter for her and the tablets. He'd supervised her work this week, asking questions and trying to understand her information, until what point?

Until she'd formed her full thesis and revealed that the archaeological ruins of an Amaran king's ancient summer palace were most certainly buried on the very same land that was about to be overturned and pulverized by Empress Oil.

As Colin asked more questions of the Secret

Service's deputy director, Ginny struggled to keep her emotions in check. Anger and horror mixed together to make her insides hurt and her eyes burn with the sting of fear-induced tears. After he hung up, he sighed deeply and stared at the phone in his hand.

"We have to go back," Ginny blurted, a dawning realization opening up a pit in her stomach. "To the museum."

Colin gaped. "You're kidding, right? Someone just tried to kill you at the museum. That's the last place you should be right now."

"No, that's exactly it. They're trying to kill me because I know something and they don't want it released. Dr. Hilden isn't actually Dr. Hilden. Who does that leave who knows about this project? Who knows the truth of the palace's location? There's only one other person who has that information."

Colin jumped up from his seat and grabbed her outstretched hand.

She passed him her keys as they ran back out to her car, Ginny's heart pounding. *Please, God...*

Colin sped back to the museum as Ginny dialed the curator's number over and over on her phone. No answer, just as the deputy director had said. She tried the front desk, but the answering machine picked up, which wasn't unusual for this time of day. The museum was small and the front desk staff often sparse. Ginny left several messages and continued calling until they pulled into the small road that split off to the museum parking lot on the left and a circular driveway up to the museum steps on the right.

Taking the driveway would get them inside the fastest and, Ginny recognized, prevent them from outdoor exposure to a potential shooter, but the entrance to the museum driveway was blocked by several police cruisers. One of the officers ran over to the hatchback as Colin rolled down the window.

The officer leaned over to look inside. "Sir, you'll need to move your—oh, hey, Tapping. You'll have to head to the parking lot or turn around. The museum's under lockdown. There was a shooter on the roof."

"I know," Colin said, exasperation in his voice. "We're the ones who called it in. They were shooting at the woman next to me. We need to get in the building. We have reason to believe the curator is in danger."

The officer shook his head and Ginny empathized with Colin's perturbed expression. "Sorry, but I'm not authorized to—"

Colin stepped on the gas and the car shot forward, jumping the curb around the police cruiser and driving onto the grass. Ginny clutched the sides of her seat as the car slammed back down onto the driveway with a bang. Shouts behind them told her they'd angered the officer. He'd probably radio their defiance to the other officers. They'd never even make it inside.

Colin pulled up to the museum steps with a screech of tires. He slammed the car into Park and jumped out his side door without turning the vehicle off, as Ginny climbed out of the passenger seat. She held her hand out and he grabbed it, pulling them both inside as two officers emerged from the building.

"Hey, you need permission to come in here," one protested as Colin elbowed past him.

"Call the chief," Colin shouted over his shoulder, yanking Ginny through the doors. "You stop us and you may be responsible for a murder."

Ginny pushed her way past several more officers who'd appeared at the doors, but no one stopped them. Inside the front atrium, a group of schoolchildren and their teachers huddled around a Baroque-style fountain, fear in the teachers' eyes as they tried their best to stay calm and cheerful for the children. The police officers guarding the children were acting chipper and answering the kids' questions about their guns and uniforms, but the responses were interspersed with wary glances around the atrium.

"Carlton! Found him?" Colin asked another officer, whom Ginny assumed he recognized from the precinct.

Officer Carlton shook his head and spoke in hushed tones. "Hey, Tapping. Checked the roof, only found expelled casings. The shooter left in a hurry and wasn't able to clean up." He pointed at the various gallery entrances around the atrium. "Our guys have checked the galleries, but there are only two other entrances aside from emergency exits, and using either of those would have set off alarms. Initial questioning rules out an inside job, as the only person here with the security code for those alarms isn't physically capable of getting up to the roof and back down here in time. Bad leg, confirmed by other staff. The front desk staff didn't see anyone suspicious come in, but the greeter here for the midmorning shift did have a rowdy visitor to deal with."

"A distraction?" Ginny offered.

The police officer shrugged. "Maybe. We'll have to check the security footage, but I don't think there's anyone in here. I suspect there never was. Shooter probably rappelled down outside or took the fire escape. Building's not too high, seems feasible."

Colin glanced back at Ginny. Her stomach lurched at the intensity of his expression. "That may be good news, Officer. Ginny?"

Ginny had felt a surge of hope at the officer's speculation, but they needed to be sure. She rushed past Colin, heading toward the curator's office. The door was locked. "Good, right?"

Colin shook his head. "No idea. Hopefully. Maybe someone called and told him to lock himself inside until the police arrived." He knocked on the door, but received no response. "We're going to have to break in."

Ginny pointed at the door handle, an antique style set inside the heavy wooden door. "That thing's ancient. I doubt it'll give you much trouble."

She watched as he shoved his shoulder against the door several times, checking its give. When it didn't budge, Colin backed up and slammed his heel into the door above the handle, again and again until the wood splintered. The door swung inward as they rushed into the room.

Ginny scanned the small office but didn't see the curator. She raced around to the back of the desk, praying she wouldn't find Mr.

Wehbe facedown like Mrs. McCall. The floor was empty, but from this angle she saw that the computer nook door stood open.

The sensation of a gentle breeze on the back of her neck barely registered as she crossed the office to the computer nook. Mr. Wehbe sat at the computer with his back to them. A wave of relief washed over Ginny. "Curator? Thank goodness, we were so worried."

As she reached the curator's side, she heard Colin's voice as though it came from far away. Whatever he was trying to tell her, she didn't hear it. All she could see was the curator's blank stare and the blood on the side of his temple. And then Colin was next to her, pulling her out of the computer room, calling for someone to get her out of there.

They'd killed him. Actually killed him. But the room had been locked from the inside. He'd been alive just a little while ago. She'd been here, in this room. Spoken with him.

Nothing made sense.

"The safe with the memory card. The backup files." She wrenched free from the police officer holding her shoulder and rushed back to Colin, who was checking the walls on each side of the curator. Looking at blood spatters?

Ginny's resolve slipped. She'd tried to stay

strong through Hilden's betrayal, the news about Empress Oil and people shooting at her, but this was too much. One more glance at the curator's lifeless form and she doubled over, losing the contents of her breakfast.

Strong hands gripped her forearms and pulled her upright into a tight embrace.

"I'm so sorry," Colin whispered. "But we've got to get you out of here. They haven't found the shooter from earlier and this door was locked from the inside. The window is open, so it's possible that's how the shooter came and left, but the police are still searching the museum and will need to secure this room as a crime scene. Let's not get in the way."

"Dr. Hilden?" Ginny's words came out hitched and hiccupped. "Do you think it was him? But Beverly Dorn was the last person we saw here."

Colin clutched her tighter and Ginny burrowed her face into his arm. She didn't want to see the officers in the room or think about what she'd just seen. Maybe she could stay here awhile, forget about everything that had happened. Let the world evaporate around them. It didn't need her anyway. All she did was get others hurt and killed, and for what? For some stupid research project?

"It's not worth it," she sputtered, voice muffled. "This isn't supposed to happen. It's not worth anyone's life."

Colin held her at arm's length and she felt an urge to wiggle free and press herself back into his arms. She shivered even though she didn't feel cold, and her mouth tasted sour from stomach acid. This was her fault. She'd taunted the man on the phone. She'd basically given him permission to do this. And she'd be next.

"I give up," she said. "I'm done. I can't be brave anymore. I did that and look what happened. He's—he was a good man, Colin. No one deserves to die, and it's all my fault."

"No. Stop that. That's just what the person who's doing this wants. If they can't kill you, they'll break you." Colin held her face in his hands. Ginny tried to hold her breath, afraid it would smell bad after her reaction to finding Curator Wehbe, but the utter inanity of being scared of bad breath when her friend had just been murdered was overwhelming and she started to laugh. Colin's intense gaze immediately blossomed into one of deep concern, creases forming around his eyes and mouth. "We need to get you out of here. I'm going to have someone watch over you while I call this in since we were first on scene. Deputy Director Bennett and Chief Black need to be notified, but I want you far away from here and under armed guard."

He didn't say it, but she saw it in his eyes—he worried that she'd do something rash. He wasn't wrong. "Find Beverly Dorn," she whispered.

Colin nodded. "We'll find her. And Dr. Hilden. One way or another, we're finishing this and we're doing it today."

He called Officer Carlton over and explained that she was to be taken out of the room and watched over until he arrived to accompany her back to the station. Something about psychological trauma. Was he talking about her? Ginny only half listened, unable to shake the image of the curator's lifeless body.

At some point, someone took her by the arm and led her away from Colin. He called to her from inside the room, but she didn't turn around. Mr. Wehbe was dead. Dr. Hilden was missing. Beverly Dorn may have been the last person to see Mr. Wehbe alive, maybe even killed him herself. In fact, she might have keys to the curator's office—maybe she'd stolen them after she'd killed him. After all, they saw Dr. Hilden leave.

But Dr. Hilden wasn't Dr. Hilden, was he?

Everything made less and less sense. Officer Carlton led her outside and radioed for one of the patrol cars at the end of the museum driveway to come and wait for her and Colin at the front steps.

"Can I sit down for a sec?" Ginny's legs shook as everything sank in. This was all her fault. What was she worth, anyway? Physically scarred, and now the project she'd poured everything into could never secure her future, not anymore. Not after all this. She'd failed.

Her body felt weak from retching in the curator's office and she craved fluids. She sat on the steps and looked up at the officer. "Do you have any water on you?"

Carlton looked back at the museum doors and then at Ginny. "If you can promise me that you won't go anywhere, I think I saw a few bottles inside the reception station at the front door. Don't move. The guys in the cruiser have eyes on you while I'm inside. Okay? You're not looking so hot."

Thanks a lot. Ginny would have found his comment amusing, under any other circumstance, but the image of Mr. Wehbe's lifeless stare and the…the…

An unmarked black Crown Victoria pulled out of the parking lot and crept along the driveway toward the museum steps. One of the officers inside rolled down his window and waved to a second marked patrol car that had started moving toward the steps. It stopped and allowed the unmarked car to make its way to her. It made sense that she'd travel in an unmarked car, especially with a target on her back.

Why had Colin stayed behind? It wasn't his job to deal with that kind of thing. He was a teacher now, a college professor. Clearly the man hadn't let go of his past, but she didn't blame him. He seemed born for the protector role, passionate and capable. He belonged in it.

"Miss Anderson?"

Ginny turned to see Officer Carlton peeking out the museum's front door. "Yes?"

"There's no water here, but I'm told there's some in the staff room. Hang on, I'll be one minute."

She nodded and turned her attention back to the unmarked car that waited at the bottom of the steps. Getting inside that car and going back to the station, what good would that do? And what about Colin? After four days with the man by her side at every waking moment, not having him here felt strange. Unpleasant, in fact.

She was about to stand up and head back inside the museum to find him when her phone began buzzing. She answered on the third ring, recognizing her TA's number. "Sam?"

"Hey, Professor A. Is this a good time?"

Ginny realized she'd been holding her breath, and was suddenly relieved to hear his familiar voice, alive and well, on the other end. When she'd seen his number, for a moment she'd feared that whoever was behind these attacks might have assumed she'd talked with her TA about her work.

"Not really, but—oh!" A sudden idea came to her. An idea that could change the tide of events for the better, perhaps give the police some leverage over whoever was conducting these attacks. "Can you go to my office? Head to my computer. I need you to log into my email and do something for me. I'll give you the password so you can find the email that was sent to Dr. Hilden and Mr. Wehbe this morning."

"Sure, Teach." Sam's voice sounded strained, as if he'd just stubbed his toe. "But I don't have the keys to your office. And I need to talk to you about something else."

Students. Ginny rolled her eyes, all too familiar with the refrain from students that they couldn't do this or that for inane reasons. "Yes, you do, Sam, and Mrs. McCall will let you in if you've forgotten your key. She should be there. She comes in on Saturday afternoons. This is really important. You'll also be able to access my accounts from the archaeology lab computer if my office isn't accessible."

"Professor Anderson, please don't—"

"Once you're in, forward that email to as many news media outlets as you can think of. The big ones. And to the journals, too, anything to do with history. Anywhere you can think of, Sam, send it and get it out there. Don't tell anyone else you're doing this. No one else in the department. Understand? Ready for the password?"

"No! Don't tell me, it's—"

Sam's response was cut off as a male voice came on the line, muffled and distorted as though he spoke through a voice-altering device. Ginny's stomach sank farther and farther as she recognized the sound from the call this afternoon.

"Thank you, Miss Anderson. Much appreciated. Your student here claimed he had access to your files, but now that I've discovered he's an uncooperative liar, I have no more need of him. You, on the other hand, have become a valuable commodity."

"No!" Ginny leaped up, phone pressed to her ear. "Don't hurt him. Please. He doesn't know anything."

"I'm afraid I can't take any chances, and he has already proved himself untrustworthy."

Ginny thought of Donna, Mrs. McCall and Mr. Wehbe. This person had tried to have her killed at least twice, and abducted once. He clearly had no qualms about harming anyone he thought might be in his way. She couldn't let that happen to Sam, too. Sam was just a kid. He had no part in this. Could she possibly bargain for his life? This had to end today. Right now.

She could not allow another person to get hurt.

"I'll give you my passwords if you promise not to hurt him." Ginny tried to sound strong and in control. "Don't you dare touch him, or I'll go to the police station and log into my email there and send my report to every major news outlet in America and Amar." She'd find Colin first. He'd know what to do.

"You do that," the caller said, matter-of-factly, "and this boy dies. Tell me your passwords now and he might live."

If she told him now, there was no way he'd let Sam walk out of there alive. There'd be no chance of getting Colin outside and down to the campus before Sam's usefulness ran out, but if she made him promise to keep Sam alive… "I'll come to you. With the passwords, in person."

The caller laughed harshly. "I'm not above

compromise. You have ten minutes. Come alone or he'll be dead before you set foot on campus. Not that I didn't expect this from you, Professor. I've already sent a car. I suggest you make use of it."

The phone went silent. Ginny stared at the device and then down at the cruiser. The caller claimed he'd sent a car? Not possible. It'd never get through the police blockade, and besides, she wasn't naive enough to get into a car sent by a killer. That meant she had ten minutes to work with. She could run and get to the campus in fifteen, but the police would certainly chase her down. Plus, it'd be foolish to go alone.

Please, God. Sam is innocent. This is all my fault. Let me make it right. She ran down the steps of the museum and knocked on the window of the unmarked car. There were two officers inside listening to the scratchy sounds of police radio chatter.

She spoke loudly to be heard over the noise. "Excuse me? Can you radio the officers inside and ask them to send Colin Tapping out? It's an emergency."

The officer in the driver's seat regarded her with calm, turned down the radio, then casually drew his gun and pointed it at her. "About time. Get in."

Ginny gasped and backed away, stumbling on the curb lip behind her. Before she could scream, the second officer climbed out of the passenger's seat. As he drew closer, something about his uniform looked wrong. As if it had come from a costume shop. "You scream and the kid dies," he growled. He waved a cellphone at her, the screen showing a connected phone call.

Frantic, Ginny looked back at the museum doors, willing Officer Carlton to return. But of course he'd take his time. He thought there were other officers watching out for her. The closest real officers—whom she presumed were in fact real—were at the end of the museum driveway forming the entrance blockade. Could she signal them somehow?

The phony officer must have caught her looking. He grabbed her upper arm with force and pulled her toward the unmarked police car. She tried to resist, dragging her feet.

"What if I refuse to come with you?"

"You hard of hearing? The boy dies. You made a deal, right? You got seven minutes now before he dies anyway. Boss gets impatient."

The phony officer in the driver's seat grunted agreement as the other guy shoved her into the front seat. "Got that right. We do all the dirty work, can't get no respect."

"Who are you?" Ginny swallowed the lump in her throat. This was no time to get emotional. If she'd learned anything from watching Colin these past few days, it was that a cool head kept a person alive. She could do this. The real officer who'd been assigned to guard her would discover she'd gone missing and tell Colin. He'd know what to do.

They drove slowly past the police cars at the driveway exit. Despite the gun pressed into the back of her ribs, Ginny tried to signal distress with her eyes. None of the officers made eye contact with her and simply waved the unmarked Crown Victoria through, which didn't come as a surprise. They thought the trouble was inside the museum. Why suspect one of their own vehicles?

When neither of her captors offered up any more information, she tried a different approach. "Where are you taking me?" Still no response, but judging by the direction they'd turned onto the main road, they were heading back to the college. "What did you do to the cops who were in this car? Or did you steal it?"

That got a laugh from the guy in the back. "You'd be surprised what you can buy at a police auction, lady. Slap an antenna on the back, add some polish and it looks like new again. We ain't no cop killers."

Incredulous, Ginny twisted in her seat. The gun pressed against her front, closer to her heart. "You've got to be joking. You know you almost shot a Secret Service agent earlier, right?"

Surprise flashed across the man's face and disappeared just as quickly. "Doesn't matter," he growled. "After this, our contract is up. Payday and off to the beaches, baby."

"Don't tell her anything," the driver snapped.

"Why not? It's not like she'll ever get a chance to tell."

"Shut *up*."

The car pulled up to the curb near the Daviau Center. The guy in the back jumped out and swung open her door with a mock flourish. "Right this way. Better hurry. You're outta time."

She tried to scan for an escape, for help, anything at all, but the campus seemed more abandoned than usual for a Saturday. And if she tried to run, what about Sam? She didn't doubt that they and their boss would not hesitate to kill.

As they led her into the Daviau Center, one more fact occurred to her. After days of using ski masks and concealing their identities, both these lackeys were now showing their faces.

Whoever had arranged this did not intend for her to get out alive.

FIFTEEN

"Sam?" As soon as they entered the department, Ginny pushed past her captors, calling for her student. Silence filled the empty space, devoid of life. Had she arrived too late after all?

"Miss Anderson," came a voice from inside deep inside the department. The male voice sounded familiar, but she couldn't place it. "I suggest you and the gentlemen who escorted you here join us in the archaeology lab."

Heart pounding, Ginny glanced toward the lab. The room looked empty from her vantage point, but that didn't mean there wasn't someone inside. The lab's L-shaped design meant not the whole room could be seen from the main entrance.

If only she could contact Colin somehow, signal her whereabouts to him.

"I'm coming. Please don't hurt Sam," Ginny

said, trying to keep her voice level. "I'm stepping inside the room now."

Her heart pounded triple time as she crossed the threshold of the lab. From this angle, she saw the cabinet where she'd originally stored the tablets, its doors still open and shelves still bare. The memory of seeing the crumbled tablets cascaded into the memory of discovering Mr. Wehbe's lifeless body. *It's all my fault,* she concluded, swallowing hard on the lump in her throat. *Maybe I'm not cut out for this job, either. Maybe my mother was right and modeling was the only job I could have been good at. But I lost my chance for that in the car crash twenty years ago. What use is a scarred girl who can't even keep her friends safe?*

She gave her head a shake. Colin had warned her that their enemy was trying to get into her head, tear down her confidence from the inside. Allowing despair to creep in would only make things worse. How many more people would have to be hurt, would have to die, before this lunatic gave up and left everyone alone?

Taking a deep breath, Ginny closed her eyes and asked for wisdom from the only one who could help her now. *Please keep Sam safe, Lord. Keep everyone safe. Give me the right words to say so that no one else gets hurt.* She stepped around the corner and her heart sank.

She'd been right after all. The false Dr. Hilden stood in front of a table at the far wall, gripping Sam by the shoulder and pressing a gun directly into Sam's temple. If he pulled the trigger right now, it would leave a little hole in same place Mr. Wehbe had been shot. Ginny swayed on her feet, but righted herself by gripping the corner of a nearby display case full of reconstructed ancient pots and ceramic shards. They didn't look like much, but appearances could be deceiving. Never had Ginny been more certain of that than in this moment.

"Who are you?" she said to the false Dr. Hilden, before shooting a glance at Sam. The boy looked scared, but not as panicked as she'd expect him to be under the circumstances. "What's going on here? Where is everyone?"

Dr. Hilden shook his head and gestured to the archaeology lab's computer. "That is not pertinent to the present situation. Miss Anderson, time to do as promised. Passwords, please. Then search the terms written on the paper next to the keyboard. Delete all relevant items from your accounts. Your student claimed he could conduct the task, but I'm afraid he oversold himself."

Ginny couldn't believe her ears. Instead of

the mild-mannered speech and Amaran accent she'd become accustomed to this past week, Dr. Hilden's voice had become gruff and American. "First you tell me who you are."

"I'm calling the shots here, Miss Anderson. Quite literally." He swung his arm across the room and fired. A clay pot on the back wall exploded into thousands of pieces. "Now do as I say or the next one will have a more permanent impact."

Ginny's ears rang from the gun going off at close range, but she got the gist of what he said. She sat down at the lab's outdated computer. It had all started to make sense: Dr. Hilden's lack of understanding about the old photograph technology, his insistence that they do everything in person. Letters composed on a typewriter. Mind games when violence didn't give him the results he wanted. The man was an old-world villain, plain and simple. She'd met plenty of people in her profession with similar attitudes toward technology. Luddites, they called themselves.

"You're all right, Sam?" She sat down and logged into her email, despite the strangeness of the task. Certainly after the meeting they'd had this afternoon, Hilden would know that she couldn't delete all of her work, as she'd sent out some emails to various publications already. Once she was in and had done as ordered, Dr. Hilden grabbed her arm and yanked her off the seat. He waved his gun at Sam, gesturing him toward the chair.

"You know what to do, boy," he growled. "No funny business. I don't trust the girl to do it." Ginny saw Sam swallow hard, then pull up a document on the screen that he copied and pasted into an empty email form. With a growing sense of dread, she watched as Sam accessed her entire academic contact list and hit Send on the email. Once it disappeared and the "message sent" notification popped up, Sam leaped off the computer chair as though burned.

"Is it done?" Hilden snapped. When Sam nodded, Hilden shoved Ginny back down into the chair. "You finish."

"Can't you do this yourself?" Ginny tried to keep her voice steady. "What do you need me for?"

"Don't you listen? I thought you were more intelligent than that, Professor." He tapped the barrel of his gun against her forehead before swinging it back toward Sam. "My employer necessitates this final step, but technology and I have a rather antagonistic relationship. I prefer doing things the old-fashioned way. Which, in this case, means delegating a distasteful task. You know your accounts best, Miss Anderson. Back to work. Time is of the essence. Show me it is done."

Swallowing hard against the lump in her throat, Ginny clicked on the Sent Mail folder and waited for the screen to load. The slowness of the old machine was excruciating, and with each moment that passed she felt certain her and Sam's time would run out. When the screen finally loaded, her heart sank. Written and sent to her entire academic email contact list was a retraction of her work on the ancient summer palace's location. She scanned the brief email, which painted her work as the ravings of a fanatic amateur who'd been using her position at Gwyn Ponth College to scam her way to fame and fortune. It made her sound crazy, unprofessional and as though her suggestion of the palace's location had about as much truth to it as the notion of aliens building the Egyptian pyramids.

It could have been written only by a professional, or at least by someone who knew the exact words to say to get her discredited. As she read the final sentences, a turn of phrase popped out that she recalled reading in one of her students' papers, time and time again. That very student now stood behind her with a gun to his head. She whirled around in her seat to see the false Dr. Hilden's gun now trained on her, and a nervous, frightened-looking Sam clutching a long billfold and an envelope.

"Are those plane tickets?" Ginny blurted as Sam stared at her, then down at the billfold. Her teaching assistant backed into a table, jostling some pieces of pottery and sending them scattering onto the floor. "Sam? You wrote the retraction? How are you involved in all this?"

"Back to work," said Dr. Hilden. "The boy is none of your concern. He has played his part and received his compensation." He flicked the barrel of his gun toward Sam. "I suggest you leave now, boy, if you have any hope of escaping the country before the police catch on."

Sam's frantic glance between Ginny and Dr. Hilden gave her hope for a moment, as she thought maybe he'd leap at the man and wrestle the gun away—but instead, Sam backed toward the lab entrance.

"Sam?" Ginny could scarcely believe it. "Sam, what's going on? You don't have to do this!"

"I'm sorry, Professor Anderson. Real sorry. But school is expensive."

"You won't be able to go to school if you're in jail, Sam! He killed Mr. Wehbe, and if you do this—" A hand clamped over her mouth.

"As I said, I suggest you leave now, boy," Dr. Hilden growled.

Sam threw one last anxious look between Ginny and Dr. Hilden, then rushed out the door.

"Sam!" Ginny screamed as Hilden's hand left her mouth. Pain blossomed in the back of her skull and sparks flew in her vision. She waited for unconsciousness to take over, but instead the pain simply throbbed. Why had he hit her with the gun? *Think, Ginny, think.*

He needed her alive for the time being, now that he'd let Sam go. It was she that he wanted, because she knew better than Sam where she'd sent and hidden all her work. But could she reason with this man? They'd spent hours together over the past week. How could she not have known there was anything wrong?

"What about us?" One of the lackeys who'd escorted her here crossed his arms in a threatening stance. "Contract's over. We did our job. Time to pay up."

Hilden turned a lazy gaze on the man and sighed, then raised his gun without hesitation.

Pop, pop.

Both men collapsed where they stood. Ginny heard screaming, far away and muffled, and then realized the screams came from her.

"Oh, quiet," Hilden snapped. "They also

oversold themselves. Technology has contributed to society's penchant for narcissism and overconfidence, it seems. They certainly didn't deserve the payday they expected."

"But you didn't have to kill them," she cried.

"Of course I did, and I'll do the same to the others once they've finished their jobs. *My* contract involves no loose ends."

And yet, he'd let Sam leave. "Sam will go to the police." Maybe if she kept him talking and didn't think too hard about the bodies only feet away from her, she could distract Dr. Hilden from what she did on the computer. If she could just send her work to even one major news outlet, and if she could recover her documents somehow—

"He won't make it out of the building alive," Hilden said. "So I suggest you stop stalling and complete the task. Eliminate all traces of your research and the palace's suggested location. Your student claimed he could do it himself, but I find myself fortunate that you managed to evade my previous efforts at your elimination. It is to my benefit that you have survived to assist with removing any technological loose ends, as inconvenient as it will now be to end this cleanly. You academic types tend to be a bit scatterbrained and your filing systems are abhorrent."

"And if I refuse? Why do I have the feeling you're going to kill me either way?"

Dr. Hilden laughed, a cruel, dark laugh that clawed into Ginny's bones. "It's your choice, Miss Anderson. Be remembered as a crazy, nut-bar academic who proposed ridiculous theories and, tortured by no one believing her, took her own life—or, leave this life with little to no recognition one way or the other. The latter option, at least, won't result in the discrediting of Mr. Wehbe's life's work for helping you on this project."

"I don't understand. Why does this matter so much? Who cares if I've found the summer palace? It's only a theory anyway, and the land has already been sold."

Dr. Hilden slammed his fist on the computer desk and leaned over, his hot, smelly breath infiltrating her senses. She clamped down on the urge to gag. "Do you have any idea what kind of money an oil company makes in one day, Professor? In a week? In a month? And do you have any idea what would happen if the Kingdom of Amar's government, or the international community, got wind of an ancient historical palace that an expert on Amar's cultural history believes is buried on the very same land that is now owned by Empress Oil? You're a smart woman. Take a guess."

Ginny swallowed as her theories took shape and became real. "Empress Oil stands to lose millions. Billions, probably, if they're not able to drill there. Work would be halted for months or even years. If I'm right and a dig team finds evidence of ancient architecture, it could be decades. Some of the ancient sites take ages to uncover properly. If the palace is as big as I think it is..."

"Billions. Tens of billions, Professor." He stood and crossed his arms. "Unless the information never reaches the public."

Ginny scoffed. "Money? This is all about money?"

"Didn't you hear? Tens of billions, in exchange for a few lives. There is no comparison." He uncrossed his arms and pointed the gun at her temple. How long had he given Mr. Wehbe before he'd killed him? She wasn't going to make it out of this one alive. She was out of options, out of time, and no one was coming to rescue her.

"You're going to kill me regardless, and if I'm dead, it won't matter what people think of me. I won't type another word."

Where was Colin? Surely he'd noticed that something was wrong by now and come looking for her. But if there were hit men outside waiting for Sam, then it was possible that Colin had run into them, too.

No. She couldn't think that way. She had to believe that she'd have another chance—that *they'd* have another chance. She saw now that she'd been a hypocrite all this time, believing herself unworthy of love because she lacked outward perfection. But she believed with all her heart that God still loved and accepted her, and she'd seen that acceptance in Colin's eyes, too.

So what if she felt afraid to let him in? If she survived this ordeal, she'd be able to face anything. Even something as terrifying as opening herself up to love.

"Time's up, Professor. Time for the next phase."

The darkness in his voice sent a shiver down Ginny's spine. "And what would that be? If you kill me, they're going to find you. Colin and the police are looking for me."

Hilden chuckled. "My dear professor, you're distressed. Your work has been discredited and the only true supporter of your work has left this life. Were I to allow you to live, surely you'd convince others that the retraction was a mistake. I and others around you, on the other hand, have witnessed the increasing distress and trauma you've faced this week with each passing incident." He leaned over, whispering in her ear. "You're a gentle soul, Miss Anderson. You've lost too much. Ah, yes, you've been a target—but with no land to dig, no curator or expert to support you, and every peer now opening their messages and reading your confession to falsifying your entire career, what do you have left to live for? Nothing. Your career is over and you have no one left who cares."

A second chill shot down Ginny's spine. She'd tried to be strong over the past few days, but it was true—even Colin had commented on how recent events seemed to be wearing her down. When she'd found Mr. Wehbe, the final reserves of her strength had drained away to the point where Colin had even had her removed from the scene. Bit by bit, Hilden had stripped away her strength and brought her to a point where it could seem plausible that she'd take her own life. "Please. Don't do this."

"Ah, but I must. At the very least, it will give me a head start. I have a schedule to keep and a job to finish."

This time when the pain blossomed in the back of her skull, it took only seconds to descend into darkness.

At the next red light, Colin abandoned Ginny's car and ran. Phone in hand, he raced as fast as he could push his legs, lungs burning even as adrenaline flooded his system. When Officer Carlton had come into the museum to tell him that Ginny and a police car were gone, he'd first thought that maybe she'd gone back to the station to rest. But Ginny wouldn't do that, wouldn't leave the scene without letting him know. They'd been through enough these past few days to know that it had to mean one thing—Ginny was in trouble.

The police at the end of the museum driveway said she'd passed in an unmarked patrol car with two officers and didn't appear to be in obvious distress. The car had turned toward the college. Colin had told them to get their heads out of the sand, get in their cars and meet him at Gwyn Ponth.

How had he even let her out of his sight? No wonder the Service had dismissed him. He hadn't been able to protect the woman he'd been assigned to, the woman he'd loved, and now it was happening all over again. He'd truly believed she would be safe with all those officers around. Of course, he'd had no way of knowing two of them were not real, but it still felt like an error in judgment. Once more, he'd stopped being perfect the moment he'd needed perfection the most.

There was only one source for help he could

think of now, and the fact that it came to mind both surprised him and didn't at the same time. He could imagine the smile on Ginny's face if she knew whom he was about to ask for help. *God, if you're listening, if you even care, give me the strength to trust you. Ginny believes you're in control. Clearly I'm not capable of being the one in control all by myself, so if you're really there, I need your help. You take point on this one.*

The crosswalk signal ahead turned to a solid orange hand. He put on a burst of speed. At the same moment, his phone began to buzz. Colin's stride faltered. Did he dare pick it up? Caller ID didn't look familiar, but what if… no, he had to pick up. He'd asked God for the strength to trust Him and needed to be open to whatever that meant. He'd never forgive himself if he didn't and it turned out to be the difference between life and death for the woman he loved.

Loved? Yes, loved. He could deny it no longer, and yet rather than feeling like a distraction, the admission motivated him even more. He would save her, whatever it took.

"Mr. Tapping?" The voice on the other end was frantic but quiet. "I think I've done a really bad thing."

"Sam? Is that you?" Colin's feet slowed to

a halt at the shock of hearing the boy's voice. "What's going on? Where's Ginny?"

"She's in big trouble, and I think it's my fault, I should never have even talked to the man and I should have known better—"

"Whoa, whoa." The student rambled on and on in a state of panic and Colin could barely make out half the words. "I can't help Ginny if you don't slow down and tell me what's going on. Pull it together. Where is she? Why is she in trouble?"

Sam's voice shook through the phone. "In the department office. There's a guy there, from Empress Oil. I thought he was Dr. Hilden, but he's not. I mean, he is? But not really. He wants Ginny to finish deleting her files, but I don't know what'll happen after."

"And you, are you safe?"

"I'm in Beverly Dorn's office. On her phone. I was supposed to leave, but I snuck back in here. Her office was open. She's not here. No one is here."

Colin's resolve turned to steel and he took off again toward the college, the sounds of police sirens close behind. "Stay put, Sam. Don't go anywhere. Hang tight. There are cops coming right behind me."

"But—"

"Backup's coming. Stay there. You're not going to get in trouble. I promise."

Colin's heart sank as the call ended, but he had to keep moving. Ginny's life depended on it.

SIXTEEN

Colin reached the Daviau Center and began his approach along the side with the least visibility from the upper floors of the building. At the museum, he and Ginny had been targeted by someone from the rooftop, and if Ginny had been led by Hilden to this building for a specific purpose, it stood to reason that someone could be waiting to ambush anyone entering or exiting.

He managed to slip inside without any shots fired, but the utter silence of the building sent his hopes plummeting. Where was everyone? He closed his eyes and took a deep breath, listening again for any out-of-place sounds.

There it was. A faint, thudding noise from afar.

"Professor Tapping?"

Colin turned to see Sam step hesitantly out of the department office. "Sam? Are you hurt?"

Sam shook his head and pointed with a

shaky hand to the end of the hallway, toward the door where Colin had entered. "He took her. She's not dead yet and I don't know where they were going, but he took her."

"Where?"

"He didn't say."

Colin grabbed the student by the shoulders and pulled him forward. "Think, Sam. Where would he go? Tell me anything you remember."

Moments ticked past as Sam stuttered through half-formed thoughts. "I don't—it's not like…look, he might—"

Colin wanted to scream, but the kid was having a rough time already. Scaring him more wouldn't help either of them. "Where's that pounding coming from?"

"Oh." Sam looked sheepish. "It's the staff from the building. An emergency meeting was called for the two departments that work in this building, but it wasn't a real meeting and Dr. Hilden had me put a cell phone signal jammer outside the room so that no one could, uh, try to excuse themselves from the meeting. I didn't ask why at the time but it's getting clearer now."

The student was culpable, but naive. Likely the false doctor had been quite convincing. After all, Ginny and the curator had worked with him all week and clearly hadn't suspected a thing. "Why? Why did he want Ginny?"

Sam's mouth opened and closed several times. "Her work. He wants to get rid of her work. I thought it was a covert operation from Amar, like checking up on us and stuff, but I didn't think anyone would get hurt."

Colin released his grip on Sam. "You thought wrong. If anything happens to Ginny…"

Sam swallowed hard and nodded. "What should we do?"

"I'm going to start searching for your professor. You're going to meet those police cars coming up the drive right now and tell them everything you told me. Then go let those people out of the meeting room."

Colin left a wide-eyed Sam staring at him in the middle of the doorway and ran outside to the quad. So Ginny hadn't been killed outright because Hilden wanted to make sure he completely destroyed her credibility. Colin was right—Hilden *had* been playing a mental game alongside the physical. The man thought ahead, planned for every eventuality. That she still lived meant he likely suspected her of having talked to someone else about her research, or maybe he thought she'd handed it off to someone else.

Either way, what value would she have after

Hilden had eliminated the possibility of other people finding out what she knew? Hilden certainly couldn't risk her returning to her work afterward. Silencing her temporarily wouldn't be enough, not after what Colin suspected he'd done to Mr. Wehbe.

Colin scanned the area around the quad, but the whole campus appeared deserted. From the corner of his eye, he spied a student racing toward the parking lot with a backpack over her shoulder.

"Hey! Kid!"

The student slowed and turned around, but continued to move away from Colin, panic clear on her face. "What are you doing here, sir? We gotta go!"

"What's going on?"

"Multiple bomb threats! Didn't you hear the sirens? We gotta clear off until the police check the campus." The student redirected her focus toward escape and ran flat out toward the parking lot.

Multiple bomb threats. A simple but ingenious way to use multiple hired thugs to get people out of the way, especially if they believed the police were still tied up at the museum. This little college town had only so many resources to draw on.

Colin sniffed, the autumn chill causing

his nose to feel stuffed up. With the deepening shadows of late afternoon, trusting his senses was getting more and more difficult. He sniffed again and paused at the arrival of a very out-of-place scent.

It smelled like someone was throwing a bonfire. On campus? That couldn't be right.

The scent of smoke grew stronger and stronger as he stood in the quad, trying to identify the direction it came from. Colin spun in a circle, a growing feeling of dread in his stomach.

And then he saw it. Tendrils of gray smoke, creeping out of the crevices of the library's upper floor. Colin raced down the path to the library and flew up the steps to the front door. He pulled on the door handle but encountered resistance. Someone had locked the door. How did Hilden get keys? For that matter, how could Hilden have managed even half of the stunts he'd pulled without unfettered access to—and familiarity with—all areas and resources of the school?

Panic welled up and a buzzing in Colin's ears threatened to erase all sense of reason. Ginny was in there. He knew, deep inside, that she was in there and she was going to die, and it would be all his fault. He hadn't protected her. He'd let her out of his sight for a moment, just a moment, despite knowing she was in danger. *Why is this happening again, God? What could possibly be your purpose for all of this?*

Colin ran his hands through his hair and tugged on it in frustration. He had to get inside. Immediately.

Most of the library's first floor was made up of floor-to-ceiling windows instead of uninviting solid walls, but the glass had to be thick. He'd have trouble breaking it, unless he took a different approach. Firing at the glass would be risky. The library looked abandoned, but there was no way to know for certain.

Colin ran across the steps to grab the nearest metal trash bin. He dragged it across the ground, bringing it to the center of the window, then stepped a few feet back into a low stance. He tensed and lifted the trash bin, beginning to swing it in a circle around him like a discus thrower making a rotation. At the apex of the rotation he released the metal bin, sending it flying into the glass window, which crunched, cracked and bowed but didn't shatter. *Almost there.*

He backed up a few more paces, and then ran full tilt into the window. At the last moment he twisted to allow his shoulder to make contact with the cracked point on the glass.

The window shattered on impact. Colin fell

into the library with a shout. His shoulder felt as if it had been knocked out of place, an excruciating pain radiating down his arm and side. *Here goes nothing, God.*

He stumbled to the nearest bookshelf, took a deep breath and rammed his shoulder into the side of the shelves. After a burst of blinding agony, his shoulder slipped back into place and the pain faded, allowing him to return focus to his surroundings.

Although he couldn't see any smoke, he smelled it.

Colin sprinted to the stairs, yanked on the red fire alarm that he hoped would summon the fire department, then kicked open the door to the stairwell.

He ran upward, the smell of smoke growing stronger and stronger as he made his way to the fifth floor. At the door, he pulled the bottom of his shirt over his nose, yanked the door open and dived inside as smoke poured into the stairwell.

The room was hot and noisy. Colin scrambled on his hands and knees toward a window, thinking to open it and gasp in fresh air. When he reached it, he remembered—the library windows didn't open, because libraries needed complete control over the building's temperature and humidity to protect the books inside. He had to find Ginny right now, before they both succumbed to smoke inhalation.

"Ginny!" Colin shouted as loud as he could, but the roar of fire grew louder and tongues of flame lapped out from between the tall bookshelves. He rushed toward flame-covered shelves, trying to squint through the thick haze of smoke to see where the fire was strongest. If Hilden had set this to eliminate Ginny and her work, that's where he'd find her.

Between the creak of weakening shelves and crackling flame, the sound of coughing spurred him toward the center of the library floor—and there she was, bound to a chair and surrounded by a stack of books and papers. Flames shot up from the documents and crept toward her shoes and pant legs. Her head lolled forward at a strange angle, but relief flooded Colin when she coughed again and tried to raise her head.

He shouted her name and their eyes met, her gaze unfocused and confused. "Colin?"

"I'm coming," he shouted, but as he made his way toward her, an old wooden bookcase in his path collapsed into a pile of burning planks and pages. His heart constricted as Ginny's coughing returned—strong at first, but weakening as he tried to pick his way around the wreckage. Adrenaline had taken him this far, but he'd already started to feel his strength waning. Breathing was becoming a chore, but giving up now was not an option.

Ginny would get out of this alive, even if it took every ounce of strength he had left. And it might. But she would live, because she deserved to. Because he refused to allow the woman he loved to perish, not again. Not this time.

His confidence waned as the heat intensified. He couldn't do it alone, couldn't save her on his own strength. He'd tried it that way before, and where had it gotten him? He'd been too cocky, too self-sure to ask for help, and the result had been tragic.

God, give me the strength to reach her in time. I know I can't do this by myself. I need you.

"Ginny?" He climbed over another fallen shelving unit to reach her chair, gritting his teeth to hold back a shout of pain from where his hand had landed. Most of the shelving units on this floor were metal, and touching the shelves covered in rows of burning books would leave at minimum a second-degree burn. He willed away the pain as he knelt in front of her, his hands scrabbling around the sides of the chair to loosen the bonds that kept her there. The knot was simple to untie, clearly tied by someone who didn't expect the hostage to try to escape.

Ginny stilled and remained unmoving as he lifted her from the chair, clutching her in his arms as he barreled toward the stairwell. He made it five steps forward before it sank in—the exit was too far away. He'd never make it there in time before he collapsed. As it was, he could barely take another breath.

The sound of shattering glass and sirens drew his attention. Sam must have made it to the patrol cars, who'd called the fire department even before Colin had pulled the alarm. Good kid. Poor decision maker, but he'd come through when they needed it most.

A bright yellow jacket filled Colin's narrowing field of vision, and his grip on Ginny slipped.

"Whoa, I've got her," the man said, reaching for Ginny. Another firefighter gripped Colin's shoulder and tried to guide him toward the window.

"I'm not letting go of her again," Colin tried to yell, coughing as smoke filled his lungs.

"You have to," shouted the firefighter who'd tried to take her from his arms. "There's no time to argue, let's go!"

But he couldn't. Not this time, not again. He stumbled forward to the window where the top of a ladder rested at the ledge. Another fire-fighter waited to carry her down the ladder, but Colin shouted at the man, determined to do it himself.

His legs gave out from under him as another shelf came crashing down to his left, the edge of the heavy frame clipping his shoulder.

He had to trust the firefighters or they'd never make it. But what if they were like the false policemen? What if they took her away again? *I trust you, God*, he finally prayed, and loosened his grip on the precious woman in his arms.

The man at the window reached in and drew Ginny toward him, slinging her carefully over his shoulder. Colin crawled to the window's edge, the last vestiges of his strength slipping away with each movement. He leaned over the lip, keeping one eye on Ginny. The firefighter reached the bottom and whisked her inside an ambulance.

Safe? Is she safe? Colin needed to crawl down the ladder, too, but darkness overtook him as he reached for the first rung.

He jolted back to awareness as someone shoved a mask over his face and commanded him to breathe. His eyes began to focus. Aluminum walls. Beeping machinery. Strange faces.

He yanked the mask off his face. "Where is she? Where'd she go?"

A gentle touch on his shoulder caused him to whirl around. "I'm right here."

He'd never seen a more beautiful sight as he gathered her into his arms and held her tight.

Ginny sat in the back of the ambulance, relieved to have Colin by her side while the paramedics fussed over things like oxygen, checking her vitals and making sure she didn't have any severe burns needing immediate attention. Truthfully, Colin appeared to have gotten the worst of it. Her head still throbbed from where Dr. Hilden—or whoever he was—had pistol-whipped her twice. The second time had knocked her out and she'd awoken only briefly to find herself tied to the chair and surrounded by a burning pile of her documents and articles before losing consciousness again. Since his earlier plans to kill her hadn't worked, it had been Hilden's new end game, his plan B to stop the world from ever finding out what she knew…and to ensure disbelief even if some piece of information fell through the cracks after her passing.

Ginny thanked God that Colin had arrived in time to prevent that. The man had risked his life to save her, and she felt as if she saw him with new eyes.

She cared for him, far more deeply than she'd ever thought she could. But was she too late? Had he saved her only out of his protector's instinct? Maybe he still saw her as an assignment, doing his duty by saving her.

Deep down, she knew this couldn't be true. They both felt something, but now was not the time. They had to finish this first.

"He's still out there," Ginny said, drawing Colin's attention from where he argued with a nurse about whether a nasty red burn on his hand needed a bandage or not. "If we don't catch him now, Empress Oil will get away with this. Someone from that company hired him, and they need to be held accountable."

Colin sat next to her, tugging at a tensor bandage wrapped around his shoulder. "Agreed, but I get the sense that it's going to be difficult to extricate ourselves from the paramedics' clutches. Plus, we're back to square one. We have no idea where he went, and without this false Hilden as evidence, accusing Empress Oil of blackmail and murder isn't going to get us anywhere."

"Maybe not."

Ginny and Colin both startled to see Sam standing outside the ambulance doors, plane tickets clutched in his hands. Ginny's shoulders tensed, remembering the moment when she'd realized Sam was in on Hilden's scheme.

Colin leaned forward and flicked his chin at the student. "Start talking, kid."

Sam held out his plane tickets and Colin took them, paging through the small packet. "I think he's planning to go back to Amar. I don't know for sure, but I do know that before Professor Anderson arrived, he said something about wanting to finish the job today so he could get paid. I assume that means going back to Amar, right?"

Ginny shook her head. "Empress is an American company. Why would he go back to Amar?"

Colin's attention snapped to her in an instant. "Because the rules are different over there. Like you said before."

"You don't think he'd go to their headquarters here in the United States?"

"We'd track and catch him there easily, and he's smart enough to plan for any eventualities. We know he's quite intelligent, based on all the interactions we've had with him. You worked together for almost an entire week and were convinced of his expertise in Amaran history. Plus, he's been trying to keep himself out of harm's way as much as possible, using hired hands to do most of his dirty work. Why would he risk being followed by the police on the off chance that he'd left a clue that leads to Empress Oil?"

Ginny rubbed her eyes with her palms, earning a scolding from a nearby paramedic. Apparently she risked scratching her eyes with any debris that might remain in or around her face. She apologized and laid a hand on Colin's knee. "But he can't just fly back to Amar from the airport, can he? We know he's not the real Hilden, so his ID can be flagged at any major airport."

"He'll have other identification. He'll be flying under his real name, most likely."

"But we'll have images of him from campus security cameras, right?" She glanced at Sam. "Can we get that?"

Sam shrugged. "I don't know how long footage is kept around. And there's no one left on campus right now due to the fake bomb threats, so it'll take a while to get the footage and, uh, isolate his image. If we even have it. It'd probably come from the library anyway, and that's kind of on fire."

Colin punched the ambulance wall in frustration, then winced in pain as the same paramedic ran over and no longer gave him a choice of whether to get bandaged up or not.

"That'll be too late. Far too late." He held out Sam's plane tickets. "Buenos Aires? Really?"

Sam shrugged. "I didn't have a lot of choice. I was going to use the money he gave me to pay off my tuition and finish the degree through Distance Education."

Distance Ed? Ginny regarded her student, normally such an intelligent and hardworking person. How had he been so easily duped? "Sam, how did he initially get in contact with you? How did you know what to do and where to go, that kind of thing?"

Sam reached into his back pocket and pulled out a folded piece of paper. "He left notes in my box in the office. Like I said, I didn't know anyone was going to get hurt. I was just as surprised as you were that he had a gun this afternoon."

Ginny took the note and unfolded it. Shock and surprise rippled through her from head to toe. Unlike the typed-up notes she'd received with the blackmail requests, this sheet was about the size of an index card and the message was handwritten. She'd seen that handwriting before, on the little notes Donna had shown her—notes that had come from Roger, the custodian.

That didn't make sense. Ginny had spoken to Roger in person before and handed off messages from Donna to him. She'd have known if Roger and the false Dr. Hilden were the same person...wouldn't she? "But the custodian has a moustache and beard, and his skin is a darker complexion. And he's always wearing a ball cap, and never seems to really look me in the eye. He's always been really focused on the task at hand." And he had an American accent. Dr. Hilden hadn't had an American accent until this afternoon in the lab.

Colin waved a hand in front of her face. "Hello? What are you talking about?"

Ginny shook the paper at Sam. "Had you ever met Hilden before today?" Sam shook his head and the pieces began to fall into place. "That's how he had access to the school, how he knew about all my research and how he knew exactly when and where to demand the drop-offs."

"Still not following." Colin stood and stretched his arms. "But if you want to fill me in, I'd appreciate it."

Ginny stood, too, grateful for the good work of the paramedics. Her headache was subsiding, and though her lungs still didn't feel totally right, she was ready for this nightmare to be over. The sooner they caught the false Dr. Hilden, the sooner there'd be justice for all the people he'd injured and killed for the sake of money. How could anyone at Empress Oil put a price on a human life? It made her sick to her stomach to think of it.

Colin must have recognized how she was feeling, because his hand squeezed her shoulder as he pulled her closer to him. "Greed makes people—and companies—do crazy things sometimes. This wasn't your fault. You did your job. You're working to make life better in that country, to preserve history and better the lives of the people there through your research. Empress Oil doesn't see that. They only see wasted potential for revenue. You can't blame yourself for that." He leaned over and kissed her forehead, and Ginny was tempted to melt into his embrace. But they couldn't afford that right now, not if her suspicions were correct.

"I think he posed as a custodian in the school," she said, drawing away from Colin. "To gain access and to keep an eye on my work. He'd have had full access to literally everywhere and everything in the college. He's probably been here for months, ingratiating himself with the staff, like…like Donna." She inhaled slowly, trying to work out what that could mean. "He and Donna left notes for each other and I thought it was a secret admirer–type situation, but now I'm not so sure. Donna really seems to like him. Remember what she told us? They were finally going to meet in person. On a date, sometime soon. He was going to call her when he was free."

Colin held Ginny at arm's length. "Where were they going to meet?"

And that's when all the pieces clicked. The conversation they'd had the other day about her plans for the date. "Colin, remember? Donna's extended family owns a small aircraft at the local airport a few miles out of the city. She has that pilot's license and was going to take him on a surprise flight above the airfield before he took her to dinner. You don't think…?"

"Absolutely I do. She's his escape plan." Colin jumped down from the ambulance, ignoring shouts of protest from the paramedics. "Send me a text message with the airport address. Sam, flag down one of the policemen around here and have them call the chief to get some backup coming behind us, but tell them to stay back and wait for my signal. If Donna's a hostage and not an accessory, this might get tricky. Tell him where I'm headed and have them warn the folks working at the airport."

"I'm coming with you." Ginny hopped down from the ambulance, too, using Colin's nearby shoulder to steady herself. "Donna's my friend, and she's already been injured once during all this mess. There's no way she's involved. And maybe if Dr. Hilden—uh, Roger—sees I'm still alive, it'll throw him off. Maybe we can use that."

Colin regarded her with a thoughtful expression, then nodded. "Fine. But you're staying in the car until I know it's safe."

Ginny rolled her eyes and pulled her car keys out of her back pocket, gripping them tightly so he couldn't snatch them away. "Fine. But for once, I'm driving."

SEVENTEEN

Not for the first time that day, Ginny marveled at how calm she felt with Colin by her side. By all rights, she should be panicking and lying in a hospital bed being treated for smoke inhalation. The latter would come once they finished this—she'd promised the paramedics she'd return for further treatment as soon as they stopped Hilden. Despite their protests, her friend's life might be on the line. Her own health could wait.

Colin's hand rested on her back as she drove, gently reminding her that she wasn't alone. When she'd woken up in the library, in the middle of the fire, she'd flashed back to the day of the car crash twenty years ago. Flames and wreckage had surrounded her then, too, and the incident had scarred her features for life. She'd managed to come out of the library fire with what the paramedics said was little more than a few second-degree burns on her legs and some singed hair, but unlike the look on her mother's face when Ginny had been pulled from the wreckage of the car crash—sporting the raw flesh of a horrific burn on the right side of her face—Colin hadn't looked at her any differently.

In fact, he'd never looked at her differently, no matter how many times she'd tried to convince herself otherwise. The only person looking at someone differently around here was herself, seeing Colin with new eyes.

Ginny knew it with full certainty. She was falling in love with Colin. She loved his sincerity, his drive to protect her and his respect for her work and for what was important to her. Not many people had been able to look past her outward scar, but he'd focused on the inside since day one. And she'd pushed him away because she'd foolishly believed her mother's words about her lack of worth.

"We're going to make it," Colin said, his voice low and even-pitched. He pointed to their left. "There's the sign for the airport. We're here?"

Later. She'd talk to him later. "Yes, but we'll have to hoof it from the front parkway, unless they've opened a gate for us to get around to the runways."

"It'll depend on whether the chief was able

to get through to anyone here and if they were able to mobilize fast enough." He pointed at a chain-link gate to the left of the departures drop-off area of the main terminal. Several trucks sat inside a garage with gaping loading bays, with no personnel in sight. "There's no one at the gate, and we don't have time to wait around. Know of any other entrances?"

Ginny pulled her car up next to the gate and put it in Park. "No, but this is a tiny airport. The aircraft are behind the garage and main terminal. It'll be faster to run around to the back and try to flag someone down from there, see what's going on."

Colin climbed out of the car and tugged on the padlock holding the gate shut. "Guess that's a local airport for you. It's up and over."

"You're not serious. The drop on the other side seems risky, Agent."

The slight smile on his face slid off at her address. "Don't. Please don't call me that."

A surprised apology leaped to Ginny's lips, but her words were lost when Colin grabbed hold of the fence and began climbing. It rattled as he moved. He glanced back at her with a frown. "Stay in the car."

He'd made it almost to the top when Ginny took a closer look at the bottom of the fence. There were several inches of clearance underneath the gate, and no tension wire along the bottom of the chain link. Colin was too large to have considered it, but she had a much smaller frame. Could she make it?

She dropped to the ground and slid sideways, sucking in deep breaths to contract every part of her body. The exertion made her realize that perhaps she should have gone to the hospital to have her lungs checked for smoke inhalation after all.

She slid her head and shoulders through first, feeling the scratch and tug of the chain link's base across her clothing, occasionally catching on her burns. Pushing through the pain, she made it through, triumphant. Hilden had been wrong. She *was* strong, despite everything. She could do this.

Colin's descent rattled the fence, so Ginny rolled away and began jogging toward the terminal. She managed to take only a few steps before a hand clamped down on her shoulder, pulling her to a stop.

"You're supposed to stay in the car."

"He tried to kill me, Colin. And my friends. This is about my work, and I'm not going to let you face it alone."

"You're not going to let *me* face it alone?"

"That's right." Ginny stepped away from his grasp and walked backward toward the path that led around the terminal and parking garage. Colin laughed, shot forward to close the distance between them and cupped her face between his hands. Her breath caught as the familiar urge to bolt returned. As the old lies tried to creep in.

He lowered his mouth to hers, stopping whisper-close before making contact. "May I?"

The lies would not win this time. She answered his request for permission without words. The urgency and danger of the moment disappeared for those few seconds as her lips met his. A thrill rushed through Ginny from head to toe as Colin's hands slid across her cheeks to find the back of her neck, twining his fingers into her hair as though afraid she'd slip away from him at any moment.

Would he stay here like this forever, if she let him? No, they both knew the weight of responsibility that fell onto this moment. She drew back from Colin as he pulled his hands from her hair. "Colin? I know this isn't the right time, but—"

He planted a quick peck on her lips and cupped her damaged cheek, cutting off her words. "You're right. It's not." Her heart sank. The disappointment and confusion lasted only as long as it took for him to draw her into a tight embrace. "I want you to feel comfortable and safe when we have this discussion, but Ginny? Whatever happens in the next few minutes, remember this. I love you. All of you. Even if you don't love all of yourself, yet."

He released her and jogged toward the airport garage, picking up speed with each stride.

With a hidden smile and determination in her spirit, Ginny followed after him. He loved her, truly loved her. She could hardly wait another minute to tell him the same, but they had business to take care of first. Still—

A bang split the air as Colin disappeared around the side of the building.

Colin ran full tilt toward the small plane at the edge of the runway, only a few hundred yards away. As soon as he'd rounded the corner of the building, he'd seen a man and woman walking hand in hand toward the airplane. He'd slowed his approach while drawing his gun to try to catch them by surprise, but there was no cover on this open airfield and he was spotted almost immediately.

The man spurred into action in an unexpected way, drawing his own weapon and firing off a shot at Colin before grabbing the woman's arm, spinning her around so that her back pressed into him as he shoved his gun into her temple.

"I wouldn't come any closer, if I were you," the man called out.

Colin slowed his steps, now close enough to see what Ginny had feared. Roger—or Hilden—had indeed duped the librarian into meeting him here, and was using her as collateral for his escape. Colin prayed that Ginny would have the good sense to stay behind the garage building. If Hilden saw that his scheme to kill Ginny hadn't worked, he might grow angry and unpredictable. Getting everyone out of here unharmed would be even harder.

Colin lowered his stance but kept his weapon trained on the false Hilden, thanking God that he'd had the courage to tell Ginny exactly how he felt before this moment. In case things didn't go down well, he'd at least leave this life knowing that she felt the same way, even if he'd stopped her from telling him in the midst of this crazy moment. She deserved better than that; she deserved a more peaceful situation where there were no pressures. No gun pointed at anyone's head. He'd be sure to take her out to dinner and give her that opportunity, just as soon as they made it out of here alive.

And they would. Saving Ginny from the library fire had reminded Colin of something—he was good at his former job. He'd been a good Secret Service agent. Despite his heart's involvement with a protectee, he'd used all his training two years ago to act the way he'd thought was right. Mistakes had been made and the results had been tragic, but that inner scar didn't need to define him for the rest of his life. *No one's scars should. Thanks for the reminder, God.*

"Let Donna go," Colin shouted, inching forward. "She's not a part of this." The librarian's expression was one of utter shock and dismay, reflecting the horror of betrayal. "She's done nothing but unknowingly help you. You should be thanking her, not holding a gun to her head."

Hilden laughed, making Colin's skin crawl. The man clearly didn't care about that; he'd been at the school to do a job—one he'd likely been paid handsomely for by someone at Empress Oil. "I'm sorry, but I can't do that. Donna has played her part well, though, hasn't she?"

"What's going on here? Roger?" The librarian looked frantically between Hilden and Colin. "What is this?"

"He's not who you think he is," Colin said. Hilden's sneer worried him. The man was cocky, believing he'd get away with this and likely become rich in the process. How much had Empress Oil paid a man like this to destroy human lives? "He's been using you for information about the school. He may have murdered the museum curator and he's the one behind the attacks on you and Ginny."

Donna's eyes grew wide as she twisted in Hilden's grasp. "No! Is this true?"

Hilden's response was to pull the gun away and plant a forceful kiss on the side of her head before returning the weapon to the same spot. "You've been a real sweetheart."

"You're disgusting," Donna growled, shifting her head slightly to face the gun barrel.

The next second, Donna spat in her captor's face and Hilden shouted in surprise, just barely releasing his hold on the librarian.

"Now, Donna!" Colin shouted. Donna pulled back her loosened elbow and plunged it into Hilden's stomach, causing the man to cry out again and double over as the sounds of sirens pierced the air.

Before Colin could run forward to pull Donna behind him to safety, Hilden raised his gun and pointed it at the librarian, finger squeezing the trigger.

"Wait!"

The gun went off, firing wildly as Hilden's attention was snatched elsewhere. Colin's heart sank, knowing full well who the voice belonged to and who'd provided the distraction.

"How are you…how did you…?" Hilden stammered, swinging his gun wildly between Colin, Donna and now Ginny.

Colin sensed Ginny come alongside him as the sirens grew louder. "It's over, Dr. Hilden, or Roger, or whoever you are." She reached for her friend, yanking Donna toward her. The librarian's face was streaked with tears. Ginny held Donna's hand, giving what small comfort she could in a trepidatious moment. "The police are on their way. You've lost."

"Not yet." Hilden trained the gun on Ginny. "I can still eliminate each of you and ensure the lovely librarian flies us out before the police arrive. You'll remain discredited, Professor Anderson. And you'll remain a disgraced former public servant, Mr. Tapping."

"It is over," Colin said. "Even if you kill us now, the police know who you are and what you've done, and we have a witness who's more than willing to testify against you. I'm sure that with a little bit of elbow grease, we can prove the connection to Empress Oil, and even if you do get on that plane and force Donna to fly you out of here? I have a feeling that not everyone at the oil company sanctioned your actions."

"The international community and the people of Amar might have something to say about this, too," Ginny piped up. "You'll have no-where to hide."

The sirens were close now, and Colin hoped that he could hold off Hilden long enough for them to get here. But the man was incredibly intelligent and resourceful. Any wrong word or movement, and this could end badly for all of them.

Hilden sighed. "I'm afraid I'll have to take my chances."

Colin leaped in front of Ginny, swinging his weapon up as his opponent's pistol discharged. At the same time, Colin fired at Dr. Hilden. The man went down, clutching his stomach. Colin stumbled backward into Ginny's arms, knowing instinctively that he'd been hit, as well.

But it had been him, not her. He'd done it. He'd saved the woman he loved, the way he hadn't been able to two years ago. He was grateful to have been given this chance to make things right—even if it meant losing his life so that she could live hers.

The sound of sirens pierced his eardrums and his vision grew hazy. Ginny's face hovered above his as he slipped toward the ground, a strange ache in his side. Tires crunched, doors slammed. Shouts of "Hands up, Secret Service!" filled the air.

They'd done it. The Service had come through for him, just as they'd promised. And this time, he'd come through for his protectee, fulfilling his own promise.

Ginny's hand caressed his cheek, the same way he'd touched hers only minutes before. Her gaze flickered elsewhere and then back to him. Strangers knelt by his side, poking and prodding at his ribs, but he didn't care. As long as he could see Ginny's beautiful face in his final moments, he could ask for nothing more.

"You did it," she said, leaning forward to whisper in his ear. "And I'm not going to wait to say it." He tried to protest, but she pressed a finger to his lips. "Not this time. After everything we've been through? I know it's happened fast, but when you know, you know. And now's as good a time as any. I love you, Colin. I love you."

Colin closed his eyes, seeing only her face, hearing only her voice as the darkness overtook him.

EIGHTEEN

Two weeks later, Ginny sat at her desk, absently tapping a pen on the arm of her office chair and watching Tigris swim circles in his bowl. She'd received a phone call this morning from the college's dean to let her know that the hearing for Sam's future at the school would be held the following Tuesday. Despite her efforts to advocate for her student, she agreed that he still needed to face the consequences of what he'd done.

She'd also managed to recover some of her professional dignity, but it would take some time to fix all the damage Hilden had done. The good news for everyone was that Dr. Hilden—or Erik Pedersen, as they'd learned was his real name—had survived the major surgery to the bullet wound in his stomach. He'd been charged and the case against Empress Oil had begun. Thanks to the cooperation of the Kingdom of Amar and UNESCO, her theorized location of the summer palace had been declared a possible historical site, and Ginny had full confidence that after the necessary parties had reviewed her work, the area would become a landmark and an important addition to Amar's cultural history and the history of its people.

Everything seemed to be working out all right, with one exception. After he'd lost consciousness at the airfield, Colin had been rushed to the hospital for surgery, too. When she'd asked the doctors about his progress, they'd told her that he'd need about two weeks before regaining minimal mobility. She'd thanked God every day that the bullet had hit only muscle alongside his stomach, unlike the wound of the man who'd shot him.

She'd visited Colin every day for the first week—though she'd had to stay in the hospital for a day of monitoring herself, thanks to the library fire and the coughing fit she'd had out of panic once Colin had slipped from consciousness—but the past few days when she'd gone to the hospital, the nurses had refused to allow her to visit his room. And he wasn't answering his phone. Had she said or done something wrong? They'd barely spoken during her visits, but that had been due to Colin's recovery. She'd been happy to sit there with him, and he'd seemed to enjoy her presence.

Had he turned out to be like all the other men who'd rejected her after all? Had he realized that he didn't want someone damaged, that someone like him who would risk his life for another human being deserved someone better? *Someone without scars.*

But, no. That didn't seem like him, not after all they'd been through and after everything he'd said. There had to be another reason. If only she could figure out what so that she could stop worrying. Her heart ached too much at the thought of no longer having him in her life.

She sighed and leaned back in her chair. Tossing the pen onto her desk, she bowed her head and prayed to the only one who could ease her worry. *Lord, I know you brought Colin into my life for a reason. If it wasn't for him, I wouldn't even be here today. I trust that your plans for the future are good, but sometimes it's hard to remember that you are in control. Please help me to lean on you first, no matter the situation.*

"Am I interrupting?" A knock on the door startled Ginny out of her moment of contemplation. Colin stood in the doorway, leaning on the frame with his arms crossed across his stomach. His eyes darted around the room, then landed back on her.

"Colin!" Ginny shot to her feet, heart pounding. "You're all right."

He nodded, his cheeks turning a light shade of pink. It was strange. She'd never seen him look so nervous before. Perhaps his wound was bothering him and he was afraid to show it?

"Sorry I haven't been very communicative lately. I had some things to figure out."

Ginny's heart sank at the graveness of his words, but she remembered the prayer she'd just offered up. Whatever came of this conversation, she'd trust that God's plans for her were good. If he'd changed his mind about her, she would simply have to accept that. "I'm so glad you're okay. I was worried. The nurses told me you'd be up and walking this week, but then I didn't hear from you and they wouldn't let me visit."

Colin moved farther into the room, but kept his arms crossed. Ginny swallowed, her throat growing dry. Normally Colin was much more animated and affectionate, so it felt strange not to have him offering a hug or a gentle touch on her shoulder.

"I've been in physiotherapy for the past few days, regaining strength so I could come over here, actually." The pinkness of his cheeks deepened as his shoulders tightened. Ginny braced for the bad news. "But truthfully, I'm tired of walking. I'd much rather kneel."

Kneel? "I'm afraid I don't understand."

He knelt on the office floor and uncrossed his arms. In one hand he held a small blue box that he opened and extended to her. Shock rippled through Ginny as she recognized what he was doing. In her office. Right now.

Inside the box sat a diamond ring in a simple white gold setting. She could scarcely believe her eyes. She met Colin's hopeful gaze, seeing her own nervousness and love and yearning reflected back at her.

"I know we—" He stopped as his words hitched. He cleared his throat and tried again. "Virginia, we haven't known each other all that long. Every day I wish, for your sake, that you'd never had to suffer through the events of a few weeks ago. But if there's anything good that's come of this, it's that it brought us together. I replay that moment at the airport over and over, wondering if there was anything I could have done differently, but if I know anything, it's that I'd jump in front of that bullet again and again if it meant keeping you safe. Lord willing, there won't be any more bullets in our future, but if there are, I want to be there stopping them for you."

Ginny could hardly speak, surprise utterly consuming her senses. She barely managed a whisper. "Oh, Colin."

Colin took a deep breath and continued. "Ginny, I've had a few weeks to think and pray, and that's been long enough for me to know with certainty that there's no one else I want to spend my life with. So, with that said… will you marry me?"

Tears pricked the corners of her eyes, and Ginny let them come. *Thank you, Lord.*

She launched herself forward, intending to hug him, but stopped herself when she remembered his injury. Instead, she joined him in kneeling on the floor, unable to keep the smile from her face. "Yes. I will."

EPILOGUE

Ten months later...

Ginny stood in her office, surveying the nearly empty room. No, she had to stop thinking of it as her office—she had a new office to finish moving into today, still inside the department but down the hall. Beverly Dorn's old office, in fact. When Ginny had been approved for the tenure-track position in the spring, the woman had packed up and left without another word.

Ginny's first act in her new promotion had been to work with the local museum and the college to establish a scholarship in memory of Mr. Wehbe. She still missed the cheerful curator, and would be forever grateful to him for giving her a chance to study the Amaran tablets. If not for Mr. Wehbe's faith in her, she might never have achieved her goal. Or had the chance to fall in love with an amazing man. God really did work in mysterious ways.

She'd miss this little office, too. It was full of memories from the events of last year, both good and bad.

"We'll make new memories," said Colin as he entered the department, seeming to read her mind. He came up behind her and rested his hands on her shoulders, then kissed her cheek and pulled her against him. "You ready to close the door and make this official?"

Ginny twisted in his grasp and wrapped her arms around her new husband. They'd waited until Colin had made a full recovery and until the media storm surrounding Empress Oil's deception had blown over before planning the wedding, which had happened on a perfectly sunny—but not too warm—June afternoon.

After returning from a brief and completely nondramatic honeymoon exploring ancient Mayan ruins, Colin had resigned his position from the college. The school had been perfectly willing to rehire him for another year's contract in the Criminology Department, but he'd admitted to Ginny that helping the local police force the year before had reminded him of what he felt was God's purpose for his life. Protecting others.

"Did you talk to the deputy director?" Ginny asked, not entirely ready to move on just yet. She held her breath, hoping for good news.

The final verdict on Colin's future at the Secret Service had been due to arrive this morning. The deputy director had been highly impressed by Colin's work in protecting her, taking down the false Hilden and uncovering Empress Oil's scheme, but unfortunately the decision wasn't solely in Bennett's hands.

Colin laughed and kissed her forehead. "You're very skilled at stalling, you know that? But yes, I did talk to him."

"And?"

Colin shrugged, and Ginny's heart broke for him. He must not have good news. "They were incredibly impressed by my work and cooperation last fall. Remember how the team from the Philadelphia field office came through for us at the airfield? Their willingness to put it on the line for me was a big deal. But Ginny, as much as I enjoyed my career at the Service, speaking to Bennett helped me to realize something."

She shook her head, bewildered. "But is that a yes or no on your job?"

"It's a yes. They offered me my position back. But I didn't take it."

It felt as though the air had been sucked from the room. She trusted he'd made the right decision, but hadn't he been waiting for this for years? "What? Why on earth not?"

His tiny smile, just for her, sent a wave of love rushing through her veins. "I'd rather stay here and build a life with you now, not years from now. There'd be a lot of travel involved if I returned to the Service, and we're newly-weds." He kissed her again, sending a thrill down her spine. A giggle escaped and she clamped her lips together to rein it in.

"Oh, Colin. If you're sure that's what you want, I'll support you. And trust me, I won't complain about having you around more often." Ginny hugged him tighter, wishing she knew the right thing to say. They'd both placed a lot of hope on Colin possibly being able to return to a position with the Secret Service, and living on only one income now would be a challenge. "I know how much you originally wanted to go back."

Colin shrugged and let his arms drop. He leaned against the door frame, looking dejected. "That's not all, though. I got a call from Chief Black this morning."

Chief Black? That couldn't be good news. What could the police chief possibly want to talk to Colin about? Her throat began to close up, anticipating terrible news. "It's not about anyone we know, is it? Please tell me nothing bad has happened."

"That depends." Colin sighed, reaching out

to stroke her cheek. "How do you feel about having a policeman for a husband?"

Her stomach dropped in surprise. "What?"

Colin's sad expression morphed into a mischievous grin. "He offered me a job. There's a position opening at the station, and while it will require some training—apparently my Secret Service training isn't exactly the same as police training—they'd like to have me on in a specialist position. Since we're not too far from Philadelphia, there's also the opportunity for promotion to a larger department in the future."

Ginny threw her arms around her husband for a second time. "That's wonderful!"

"And that's not all."

Could her heart handle any more? Having Colin work on the police force would be quite the change—and of course she'd worry about him every single day while he was on duty—but protecting others was the desire of his heart. He'd been right, that afternoon last October when they'd shared their first kiss. Everyone had scars, whether inside or outside, but no one needed to live a life defined by them.

He hadn't let his mistake stop him from pursuing a return to the job he was born to do. And Ginny, with his encouragement, had reached out to her mother and sent her a wedding invitation. She hadn't come to the wedding, but she'd phoned to offer her congratulations. Ginny had been surprised to discover how much that simple gesture had meant to her. It was a start to reparations.

"Don't tell me, you're also going to work part-time at the doughnut shop?"

Colin grinned again. "Close your eyes."

"I'm not sure I like the sound of that."

"Trust me." He took her hand and led her out of the office. "Close your eyes for a minute."

Biting back a witty retort, Ginny did as he asked and allowed him to lead her. They didn't walk far before stopping. She heard the sound of a door being unlocked. "Colin, that wasn't very far."

"I know. We just had to get to your new office."

Ginny was tempted to open her eyes and glare at him. "It's being painted! We're not supposed to open the door until the fumes are gone. Mrs. McCall is highly sensitive to chemical smells. It's why the window is open instead."

"The smell has been gone since this morning, Ginny. You just didn't notice or check because you've been teaching classes all day. You can open your eyes now, though."

Ready to scold him for acting ridiculous,

Ginny opened her eyes. She gasped. On the far side of the room, a large cabinet aquarium had been set up. At least fifteen gorgeous tropical fish swam inside, flitting among aquarium decorations set up to look like ancient ruins. A low rumble from the tank told her it had been set up properly, with filtration and heating and everything tropical fish needed to thrive.

Ginny was speechless.

"Do you like it?" Colin's excitement had notably diminished, replaced by worry. "I did have to get special permission from the school to put this in here, but I'd hoped—"

With a heart full of gratitude and joy, she wrapped her arms around her husband yet again and rested her head on his firm chest. "It's perfect, Colin. Thank you. I don't know how, but you always seem to anticipate what I need before I even know I need it."

He kissed the top of her head and Ginny shivered with happiness. "It's because I love you."

"I love you, too," she whispered, knowing full well that since the first day they'd met, and despite everything they'd been through, God had been in control. And always would be. "I love you, too."

* * * * *

Dear Reader,

If there's one thing most of us struggle with on a daily basis, it's our appearance. Right? Our weight, our height, our features…too big, too small, wishing we had curly hair or straight hair or a different complexion. Ginny's car accident left a lifelong scar that caused her to struggle with feelings of low self-worth, and she needed to learn that true self-worth comes from the inside. We are all precious and beautiful in God's eyes—He looks at the heart, and that's where we should place our focus. Then our inner beauty can reflect outward, and what's lovelier than that?

And I know you perfectionists in the crowd (me too, me too…) identified with Colin's anguish over what he perceived as a moment of failure that would forever define him. But we all make mistakes. We have to own them and learn from them, and accept what God teaches us through those moments. It's easier said than done, though—it's a lesson I'm constantly re-learning.

While the Kingdom of Amar and the Ashmore Museum are fictional places, the Ashmolean Museum in Oxford with its massive collection of ancient tablets is not. I love ancient history, and I hope you enjoyed this suspenseful spin on its study. Thankfully, the job usually isn't so fraught with danger—or so my friends working in the field tell me!

I love hearing from readers. To contact me, visit michellekarl.com or find me on Twitter, @_MichelleKarl_. Thank you so much for reading *Unknown Enemy*!

Blessings,
Michelle

LARGER-PRINT BOOKS!

GET 2 FREE
LARGER-PRINT NOVELS
PLUS 2 FREE
MYSTERY GIFTS

Love Inspired®

Larger-print novels are now available...

LARGER-PRINT BOOKS!

GET 2 FREE
LARGER-PRINT NOVELS
PLUS 2 FREE
MYSTERY GIFTS

Love Inspired®

SUSPENSE
RIVETING INSPIRATIONAL ROMANCE

Larger-print novels are now available...

REQUEST YOUR FREE BOOKS!

2 FREE INSPIRATIONAL NOVELS
PLUS 2 FREE MYSTERY GIFTS

Love Inspired® HISTORICAL

YES! Please send me 2 FREE Love Inspired® Historical novels and my 2 FREE mystery gifts (gifts are worth about $10). After receiving them, if I don't wish to receive any more books, I can return the shipping statement marked "cancel." If I don't cancel, I will receive 4 brand-new novels every month and be billed just $4.99 per book in the U.S. or $5.49 per book in Canada. That's a saving of at least 17% off the cover price. It's quite a bargain! Shipping and handling is just 50¢ per book in the U.S. and 75¢ per book in Canada.* I understand that accepting the 2 free books and gifts places me under no obligation to buy anything. I can always return a shipment and cancel at any time. Even if I never buy another book, the two free books and gifts are mine to keep forever.

102/302 IDN GH6Z

Name	(PLEASE PRINT)
Address	Apt. #
City	State/Prov.	Zip/Postal Code

Signature (if under 18, a parent or guardian must sign)

Mail to the **Reader Service:**
IN U.S.A.: P.O. Box 1867, Buffalo, NY 14240-1867
IN CANADA: P.O. Box 609, Fort Erie, Ontario L2A 5X3

Want to try two free books from another series?
Call 1-800-873-8635 or visit www.ReaderService.com.

* Terms and prices subject to change without notice. Prices do not include applicable taxes. Sales tax applicable in N.Y. Canadian residents will be charged applicable taxes. Offer not valid in Quebec. This offer is limited to one order per household. Not valid for current subscribers to Love Inspired Historical books. All orders subject to credit approval. Credit or debit balances in a customer's account(s) may be offset by any other outstanding balance owed by or to the customer. Please allow 4 to 6 weeks for delivery. Offer available while quantities last.

Your Privacy—The Reader Service is committed to protecting your privacy. Our Privacy Policy is available online at www.ReaderService.com or upon request from the Reader Service.

We make a portion of our mailing list available to reputable third parties that offer products we believe may interest you. If you prefer that we not exchange your name with third parties, or if you wish to clarify or modify your communication preferences, please visit us at www.ReaderService.com/consumerschoice or write to us at Reader Service Preference Service, P.O. Box 9062, Buffalo, NY 14240-9062. Include your complete name and address.